Once in a Lifetime

The Vineyard Sunset Series

Katie Winters

Chapter One

There was something about peak wedding season on Martha's Vineyard.

Any given Saturday, a cacophony of wedding bliss echoed across Oak Bluffs. Rice was tossed, as were tiny flowers. Brides and grooms latched hands, their smiles enormous as they leaped into their rented convertibles and drove off— a banner with JUST MARRIED fluttering behind them.

It was a season of hope, prosperity, and first, second, and third chances. Anyone who believed in the beauty of falling in love couldn't resist it.

Charlotte Montgomery Hamner was a seasoned wedding planner, and because of this, there wasn't a whole lot she hadn't seen over the years. She'd been at the helm of everything from a wedding between two eighty-five-year-olds (who'd found one another again sixty years after a breakup) to a wedding between two eighteen-year-olds who couldn't wait to get their lives started. She'd seen break-ups ten minutes before the aisle walk and reunions five minutes later. She'd seen mothers

1

absolutely lose their minds with sorrow, terrified that their sons were marrying the wrong women. She'd seen mothers lose their minds with happiness, so grateful their sons were finally settling down. She'd seen dog, cat, parrot, and hamster ring-bearers and had even served as a stand-in bridesmaid herself when the original bridesmaid had run away with the bride's stepbrother just before the ceremony. The bride had even let her keep the dress.

Charlotte's career had since skyrocketed after that fateful November nearly two years ago, when she'd been hired to plan the last-minute wedding ceremony for Ursula Pennington and her NBA basketball player fiancé. That wedding had come with a fair share of heartache and panic. Most notably, the bride had almost not walked down the aisle at all.

Lucky for Charlotte, Ursula had walked down that aisle. That single event had brought on an avalanche of popularity for Charlotte's wedding planning business. Since then, Charlotte had worked for celebrities, the thirteenth-in-line for the English crown, and the daughters of billionaires. She'd been written up in countless wedding magazines, cited as the "one to hire for your Martha's Vineyard wedding." Other wedding planners resented her, while many others admired her. This solidified in Charlotte's mind that she'd made it.

It was August 6th at six-thirty in the morning— smack dab in the middle of wedding season. A large coffee pot filled itself in the corner of Charlotte's kitchen as she stood in a yoga pose, her eyes closed while she balanced on a single foot. Outside the house, a seagull squawked, destroying her meditation.

"Wow. Was that a pterodactyl?" Everett's footfalls

were soft across the hardwood kitchen floor. He grabbed the pot of coffee and filled his mug, smiling at Charlotte.

"It's *Jurassic Park* all over again," Charlotte told him, placing her foot on the ground to steady herself. "Better watch out."

"And here I thought that the only thing to watch out for today was 'bridezillas,'" Everett teased.

"Funny, Everett."

For perhaps the millionth time, Charlotte nearly burst with how handsome his smile was. How had she gotten so lucky? Slowly, she crept one foot back to the hollow behind her knee and attempted her yoga pose once more. A split-second later, she lost her footing and teetered. Everett and Charlotte shared the joy of this silly moment, their stomachs bouncing with laughter.

Photographer Everett had been yet another gift from that Ursula Pennington wedding a couple of years back. He'd been hired as an event photographer for the big event and had been instrumental in keeping Charlotte above water throughout the chaos.

Somewhere along the way, they'd fallen in love.

This, most especially, was incredible for Charlotte. Love hadn't been in the cards for her. Not after her husband, Jason, had died in a fishing accident nearly three years ago. Jason had been the love of Charlotte's life, the father of her only child, and so much more. He'd been a thief of good snacks, an endless teaser, and an incredible lover. He'd loved sci-fi movies, long runs in the rain, and being out at sea with the wind sailing them home. He'd filled her life with song and purpose, and his death had nearly stripped it of all its joy.

Yet, for some reason, one that Charlotte didn't completely understand, her heart had allowed space for another love. She couldn't have been more grateful or more surprised.

Everett poured Charlotte a cup of coffee and beckoned for her to sit at the kitchen table with him. "I think your yoga time is over." She did, using her elbows to prop her chin up and heaving a sigh. Outside, another seagull squawked again, making fun of her.

"You didn't sleep, did you?" Everett asked.

"Not that much."

Everett's dark eyebrows furrowed. "What did she have you re-do this time?"

Charlotte shrugged. "Pick something. The cake? The seating arrangements? The music? I've had to plan and re-plan everything four or five times at this point."

"Does she know that it's supposed to be her wedding and not a 'torture Charlotte extravaganza'?" Everett joked.

"I'm not sure if she got the memo."

Rachel appeared in the doorway, rubbing sleep from her eye with a fist. She wore an oversized Oak Bluffs High School t-shirt and a pair of basketball shorts, and her hair had been disheveled into a weird mass from her pillow. She reached into the fridge and grabbed the carton of orange juice, grumbling a "Good morning."

"Hi, honey," Charlotte replied. "How did you sleep?"

Rachel, who was seventeen and about to enter her senior year of high school, collapsed on the third kitchen chair and poured herself a glass of juice. "Doesn't matter," she returned, like a soldier on the front lines. "Let's go over the list of what we need to do this morning."

The corners of Charlotte's lips quivered into a smile. Everett laughed. He reached for the newspaper and stretched it out in front of him. "Carry on," he said as he flipped to the sports section. "No talking any sense into either of you. That bridezilla has full control."

Charlotte retrieved her cell phone and propped it between herself and Rachel. There, she'd outlined the list — the items they needed to pick up for the ceremony and reception, when they planned to meet the bride and her bridesmaids, what time the string quintet planned to arrive for the pre-ceremony drinks and hors d'oeuvres, and on and on. Charlotte and Rachel were accustomed to the never-ending list of wedding responsibilities.

This particular Saturday felt different, though. This was because the current bride, Felicity Villman, was one of the worst women they'd ever met. Period.

Charlotte and Rachel showered, did their makeup, and dressed in black dresses with their hair curled to perfection across their shoulders. They met at Charlotte's car, groaning with fear about the day ahead.

"She's going to send us on non-stop errands all day long," Rachel said as she buckled her seatbelt.

"Maybe I'll tell her that the time for changing her mind is finished. She can't do it anymore," Charlotte tried.

Rachel coughed with doubt. "Yeah. Right."

"You're right," Charlotte moaned. "She's paying us too much money not to fall all over her. Gosh, it's just a shame. Normally, this job is so fulfilling. You get to watch someone celebrate their love and prepare for the rest of her life."

"Maybe this is the way Felicity wants to celebrate," Rachel pointed out.

Felicity Villman was the daughter of an importer-exporter who supposedly made a little bit more money than God. She was her daddy's treasure, which had resulted in a sort of "My daughter will get anything she wants for her wedding" vibe. This was ordinarily a good thing for Charlotte, who was happy to prepare beautiful weddings, blowing past traditional cost boundaries. With Felicity, however, there was absolutely no joy. It was all pain.

And in truth, she wasn't sure she thought the bride and groom had any love between them at all. She hadn't said anything about this to anyone, not even Rachel. That was the sort of thing a wedding planner kept to herself.

The first stop on their all-day Saturday mission led Rachel and Charlotte to Claire's flower shop. Claire was Charlotte's sister and dearest best friend, a woman who'd been there for Charlotte through thick and thin (and gosh, there had been a lot of thin). Claire was Charlotte's right-hand woman for all things wedding, as her artistry led her to make gorgeous bouquets for every wedding arena. There were bouquets for the bride and the bridesmaids, flower arrangements for the ceremony and the reception, plus corsages for important women relatives and bouton-nieres for the men.

Claire greeted them from behind a mess of flowers and twigs. Petals lined her hair, not on purpose but through the flurry of activity of perfecting each and every bouquet. She held Charlotte a little too long and dusted a bit of soil across the shoulder of Charlotte's dress.

"How's our Felicity doing?" Claire asked.

"She just texted me that she woke up," Charlotte replied, wrinkling her nose.

"Oh, good. I hope she updates you with every single

step of her morning. When she blows her nose or when she..." Claire began.

"Claire..." Charlotte warned. "We won't get through this day any better with bad attitudes."

"She keeps telling me that, too," Rachel said, sticking out her lower lip with disdain.

Claire chuckled, then flung up her hands. "All right. Well. All your bouquets are finished. The boutonnieres and corsages are in a box. What else?" She bustled around, counting out the unique creations she'd made. "Let's bring them out to your car. You said you'll be storing them in the walk-in fridge at the hotel?"

The wedding itself was held at The Quarry Estate outside of Chilmark, a drop-dead gorgeous establishment offering a glittering view of the water just behind the cliffs. Charlotte had initially wanted to propose that Felicity marry her groom at the Aquinnah Cliffside Overlook Hotel, which her sister, Kelli, had been redesigning for the previous year. Unfortunately, the Aquinnah Cliffside Overlook Hotel needed several more months of redesign, and Felicity's wedding had to be moved to an alternate location. Charlotte knew that Kelli was secretly gleeful about this. Felicity's wedding was something of a stain on the entire island. Nobody liked her energy.

She was like a villain in a Disney movie. All the good people of Martha's Vineyard didn't like her. They didn't carry this dislike over to Charlotte, thankfully. They just prayed for a day when Felicity left the island for good instead of hanging around, leaving bad reviews online for otherwise wonderful restaurants, and making shopkeepers' lives difficult.

* * *

Around noon, Rachel and Charlotte parked outside The Quarry Estate and watched as the bride and her much shorter mother bickered in the parking lot. The bride wore a white onesie, a shiny tiara, and a pair of flip-flops. She looked ridiculous, especially as her face contorted with anger.

"What do you think they're talking about?" Rachel asked softly.

"Maybe they're talking about how it's a beautiful day for a wedding," Charlotte tried, just as Felicity stabbed her finger through the air to make a point. It was terrifying to watch.

After Felicity and her mother bounded inside, Charlotte and Rachel waited in the car, fearful, for a good five minutes. When they finally entered the building and headed toward the quarters they'd rented for Felicity and her bridesmaids to get ready in, their breathing was coming in ragged and strange.

"Let's face the music," Charlotte whispered to her daughter.

But when they opened the door to the dressing room, laughter spilled out. There before them, Felicity and three of her bridesmaids sat in front of mirrors as makeup artists prepared their faces. Felicity's mother gabbed and gossiped in the corner, happy as a clam. Charlotte, who'd basically imagined Armageddon on the other side of the door, tilted her head with confusion.

"Hi!" Felicity greeted, waving both hands. "She's here, everyone! My brilliant wedding planner! You know, she also did Ursula Pennington's wedding."

The other bridesmaids blinked their very long and fake eyelashes toward Charlotte. Charlotte waved in greeting and bent down to Felicity (but not too close). Her perfume was a powerful cloud.

"How's your big day going so far?" Charlotte wasn't sure if the smile she now presented Felicity looked fake or overwhelming, or both. For a moment, she regretted saying anything at all.

But a split-second later, Felicity just said, "Oh, it's been wonderful. The girls surprised me with green juice and champagne in the room. Hard to believe it's my final day as a Miss!"

"Harvey doesn't know what he's got in store," one of the bridesmaids said mischievously.

Charlotte wondered if the bridesmaid said this out of love for the bride or out of fear for the bride. Perhaps it was both.

As the bride was buttoned into her dress and the hair and makeup was finalized, Charlotte and Rachel rushed around the reception hall, the exterior gardens, and the place where the ceremony itself would take place. One hundred white-painted chairs had been set up on a lush green lawn, pointed toward the water. Charlotte pinched herself as a reminder that this was actually happening.

"There were so many times I thought Felicity would call today off," she explained to Rachel.

"There were so many times I thought you would quit this wedding," Rachel countered.

"But she seems almost happy? Dare I say that?" Charlotte asked.

"You can. I think you're right. Maybe she was just nervous about everything and didn't know how to talk about it," Rachel tried.

Charlotte stopped and made a small note to herself on

her clipboard. She then spoke into her headset to discuss something with the arriving caterers, who would soon begin to prepare the first hors d'oeuvres for the pre-ceremony cocktail hour. Charlotte felt strength in her voice, proof that she'd battled her way through difficult weddings before. There was no reason she couldn't do that again.

When that call finished, she locked eyes with Rachel. The mother-daughter duo shared a smile.

"Let's get this show on the road, shall we?" Charlotte asked.

"No time like the present," Rachel quipped. "Let the games begin!"

Chapter Two

Charlotte stood behind a double-glass door, her hand pressed against the shoulder of the lead flower girl and her ears perked. Behind her, all five bridesmaids, the bride, the mother of the bride, and the billionaire father of the bride waited for their cue. The air was heavy and expectant. Even the gossiping bridesmaids had taken the hint that it was time to listen, not speak.

Across the lush lawn, one hundred guests sat in wait. An opera singer soared through a gorgeous solo, her eyes closed and her hand across her heart. On the other side of the chairs, Rachel stood, watching the crowd from a different perspective and ensuring everything went smoothly. Just as soon as the opera singer decrescendo-ed, Rachel pressed her earpiece and whispered, "Okay. Everything is clear over here. Are the flower girls ready?"

"We have the flower girls all prepped and ready," Charlotte whispered into her headset. Rachel lifted her thumb in response.

The string quintet began to play "Pachelbel's Canon."

With trained ease (because she'd come to the estate herself and practiced it over and over again), Charlotte stepped up and opened the double-wide doors. She then directed the first flower girl down the grassy aisle, watching as she tossed her petals to the left and then the right. For a four-year-old, you had to hand it to her. She was doing a fantastic job.

Next, Charlotte directed the bridesmaids down the aisle. "Remember. Keep your chins up and your shoulders back. Smile, smile, smile. It's a happy day." She sounded like a kindergarten teacher.

Finally, the bride stepped forward, arm-in-arm with both her mother and her father. Often, that kind of thing brought tears to Charlotte's eyes. It made her ache to think that Rachel would only have Charlotte on her wedding day; her father wouldn't make it.

What role would Everett play? Oh, it didn't matter, now. Charlotte shoved that thought away.

"You ready?" Charlotte asked the bride, her smile straining her cheeks.

The bride nodded, blinking back tears. She no longer looked like the alienating monster from the previous several weeks. It was hard to imagine that, just last week-end, she'd tortured a waitress at a seaside restaurant so much that she'd had to be sent home, crying. Well, that was the rumor, anyway.

"Thank you for all your help, Charlotte," she sniffed. "This is truly the happiest day of my life."

So often, brides told Charlotte that. But this time, perhaps because it was such a contrast to Felicity's normal personality, Charlotte really took it to heart.

"I wish you all the happiness in the world," Charlotte

told her, really meaning it. "Go out there and get your man."

* * *

After the photographs were taken and post-ceremony cocktails were drunk, Charlotte guided the guests into the reception hall. The hall itself was old-fashioned, with hanging chandeliers, ornate golden clocks and statues, and round tables with white tablecloths. When Felicity had first seen the place, she'd squealed and said, "Oh, I love it. It's just like *Titanic*."

Along the side of the hall, floor-to-ceiling doors opened out to a beautiful outdoor garden, where they'd decided to set up the dance floor and the live band. As the guests entered the reception hall, the live band began to play a blues-style version of "Just the Two of Us." Charlotte had to admit that it wasn't half bad.

As Charlotte headed to the kitchen to check on the cake, Rachel buzzed past her en route to check on something else. Discretely, they lifted their hands and high-fived each other.

"Is it my imagination, or are we killing this?" Rachel whispered.

"It's one of the best weddings I've ever seen?" Charlotte muttered back, at a loss.

Charlotte popped through the swivel door between the hall and the kitchen. Back there, several line cooks and a head chef finished plating the first salad course, upon which they placed a healthy slab of pink salmon. Charlotte waved a hand and complimented the hors d'oeuvres. "I managed to grab a crab cake," she explained.

"And it was to die for! I knew there was a reason I always recommend you guys to my clients."

The chef saluted her and returned to work, his face stoic. Charlotte knew better than to try to joke with the chef and the kitchen staff. Theirs was a tough and quick-paced job. Yes, hers was too, but it required a whole lot more "fluff" and a whole lot less "slicing, dicing, sautéing, boiling, and plating." They didn't have time to talk.

Rachel and Charlotte had retrieved the cake from renowned cake decorator and Charlotte's first cousin, Christine Sheridan, earlier that afternoon. The result was a knockout— ten tiers with delicate fondant flowers and fondant "lace" around each tier. A classy-looking wedding topper stood at the top, the bride and groom old-fashioned and regal.

Sure, the whole "cake decision" had been a difficult one. Felicity had gone back and forth on the topic, some-times calling Charlotte in the dead of night to declare that she "hated" the old cake idea and had a brand-new idea. This particular cake design was simplistic yet honorable, not the sort of thing anyone could fuss about.

Rachel came through on the speaker of Charlotte's headset. "How's it looking?"

"Just like it did when we brought it in," Charlotte returned.

"Fantastic. I have a small issue out here with the seating arrangements. Seems like an ex-wife of someone doesn't want to sit with the ex-husband's new step-daughter."

"I'll be out in a sec to handle it," Charlotte affirmed.

"No need. I have an idea," Rachel told her.

Charlotte's heart lifted. Over the previous couple of years, Rachel had really stepped to the plate in the wedding industry, especially during "peak wedding season," which just happened to be between school years. Charlotte often imagined how much further ahead she'd have been if she'd gotten into the business at Rachel's age. If Rachel wanted to, she could strike up her own business in a few years and already advertise herself as having eight years of experience.

Out on the islands of Nantucket and Martha's Vineyard, wedding planners were a hot commodity. There would certainly be brides for the taking.

* * *

Dinner was plated and served. The blues band continued to play; the music rang out through the open glass doors and filled the old-fashioned world with a hint of the new one. The gorgeous crowd chatted amicably, with their drinks lifted and their forks tinging their plates. At the head table, Felicity and her groom, Harvey, seemed lovey-dovey, frequently leaning in to kiss one another, just like a bride and groom were meant to.

After the meal, the lead singer of the blues band announced that it was time for the "first dance." This, Charlotte remembered, had also been a bone of contention for Felicity, who'd said that a "first dance" was usually lame and often boring for the rest of their guests. Eventually, however, she'd called Charlotte to request "Close to You," originally sung by The Carpenters. Charlotte found this to be a strangely adorable choice, especially coming from someone she often feared for her life in front of. She passed the news along to the blues band, who concocted a near-perfect blues rendition.

As Harvey and Felicity danced across the dance floor,

their guests gathered, snapping photographs and watching as Felicity tilted her beautiful face toward Harvey's and whispered words they couldn't hear. Charlotte marveled that, actually, Felicity was a whole lot more beautiful when she was smiling rather than insulting whoever was around.

Mid-song, Charlotte and Rachel hustled back to the kitchen to retrieve the cake. They wheeled it out to the corner of the dance floor, positioning the bride-and-groom topper so that they looked out across the crowd. The song finished, and Felicity and Harvey shared a tender kiss as the crowd around them howled.

"Maybe I do believe in true love," Rachel said under her breath.

"Why the heck wouldn't you?" Charlotte shot back. She wanted her daughter to believe in all beautiful things, big or small.

Felicity remained on the dance floor with several bridesmaids, all of whom gushed about the wedding. Felicity flipped her hair behind her shoulder as the blues band started to play. One of her girlfriends grabbed her wrist and bobbed along beside her, dancing in her outrageous heels. Felicity stumbled slightly and fell off to the side. There was a sudden hush across the dance floor. Charlotte's heart stopped beating for two full seconds.

There was a rip. The wedding dress had caught beneath the heel of her shoes and ripped a full three inches.

Charlotte gaped at the gash with horror and tried to drum up something to say to calm Felicity down. The last thing she wanted was for Felicity to suddenly scream at her friend in the center of the dance floor. Nobody liked a demonic bride.

When Felicity lifted her gaze, she directed it toward Charlotte, of all people. Her lower lip quivered with rage. She then dropped her eyes toward the cake. A look of horror was transfixed across her face, as though the cake itself was made of fire.

"What the heck is that?" she demanded, her voice low.

Charlotte's eyes widened. She turned to blink down at the cake, which was the exact one Felicity had asked for. "Um. It's your cake?"

Felicity lifted her dress as she staggered forward. The ripped edges frayed in the breeze as she moved forward. "That is not my cake."

Charlotte's throat tightened. She took a hesitant step back, keeping a smile on her face. The last thing she needed was for the crowd to notice this meltdown.

"This is the cake you asked for," she said.

Felicity's nostrils flared. Here she was, the Felicity that Charlotte knew so well. "This is not my wedding cake. I need you to take it away and get me a new one."

Charlotte wanted to laugh. She wanted to fall to the floor, tear at her own dress, and roll around the reception hall, wailing with laughter. The entire situation was crazy.

"Where do you suggest I get a wedding cake five minutes before it's time to serve it?" Charlotte asked flippantly.

Felicity's cheeks were blotchy with rage. But just as she opened her mouth to tear into Charlotte, the groom appeared. He leaped for Felicity and pressed a hand on her shoulder. Felicity shook his hand off and pointed at the cake, enraged.

"Harvey. Do you see what she's done?"

Harvey's eye roll was so deep that he nearly lost his eyes in the back of his head. "Felicity?"

"Because, Harvey, we've paid this woman a lot of money, and I mean a lot, to make our day perfect. Don't you want our day to be perfect?" Felicity continued.

A few people along the edge of the crowd had begun to notice Felicity's anger. Charlotte nibbled on a finger-nail nervously. She was terrified of what would happen next. She remembered how much Felicity's father still owed her for the rest of the fees. It wasn't a number to sniff at.

"Felicity?" Harvey's voice meant business. It was like a teacher calling out a misbehaving student in class.

Felicity blinked at her new husband. All the color drained from her cheeks. "Harvey, if you disagree with me, I—"

But suddenly, Harvey's massive hand flashed back into the cake. He ripped a massive chunk from the tenth tier, directly below the husband-and-wife topper, and then he smashed the cake directly into Felicity's mouth to shut her up.

Charlotte had never seen anything like it, not in all her years of working as a wedding planner.

Those who'd noticed the fight gasped at the sight of the bride, dripping with cake. Those who hadn't noticed, however, just assumed that this was all a part of the fun. It was a classic event in most weddings— the husband and wife shoving cake between each other's lips. She was sure it was romantic to some and then not so much to others.

Felicity gaped at her husband for a long time. Vanilla frosting dripped from her lips. Harvey let out a single, hesitant laugh as though he'd just decided to stand up to a bear. *You didn't just decide to stand up to a bear. There were rules in this life.*

But before Harvey could run, Felicity leaped forward, grabbed a mound of cake for herself, and shoved it against Harvey's mouth. The crowd adored the scene and howled. Even the blues band began to play "Top of The World," another Carpenters' song, which lifted the mood considerably.

In fact, a split-second later, Felicity pressed her head adoringly against Harvey's chest and whispered up at him. "I just lose my cool sometimes, Harv. You know that."

"I do. I do know that." Harvey spoke like someone who'd been to hell and back. Still, his eyes reflected sincere love.

The issue of the cake was soon forgotten. Charlotte sent it back to the kitchen to be sliced and plated, and soon, the guests were enjoying Christine Sheridan's masterpiece. Charlotte and Rachel both nabbed pieces of their own and ate them secretly in the hallway, gobsmacked at the turn of events.

"Felicity really loves him," Rachel offered, licking the tongs of her fork.

"And he seems to really love her. And know exactly what to do to calm her down," Charlotte muttered.

"He better have a lot of cake on-hand over the years," Rachel said.

"I wish him luck," Charlotte said. "She's terrifying."

Rachel and Charlotte peered through the window of the reception hall, watching as Felicity tossed her head back joyously, her arm wrapped around her husband's waist. There was still a tiny bit of frosting in her hair. Nobody would tell her because they were too afraid.

Chapter Three

Charlotte drove bleary-eyed back to the house, her knees screaming and her once-curled hair limp and ragged. Rachel chatted excitedly beside her, fluffing her curls as the radio spit out pop music. It was ten at night, and they'd just said goodbye to the catering staff, put the wedding guests in taxis, and watched the bride and groom walk barefoot and drunkenly hand-in-hand toward their wedding suite. Just before his own departure, the father of the bride had slipped a two-hundred-dollar tip into Charlotte's hand and told her he would "pay the rest of the bill first-thing Monday morning." Charlotte could have cried with relief.

The red-bricked house sat up a bit from the Vineyard Sound and had a wraparound porch and large bay windows that often seemed to suck the light in from the gorgeous summer surroundings. Everett and Charlotte had purchased the place when they'd decided to move in together, leaving behind the home where Charlotte and Jason had raised Rachel together. It had been a heartbreaking yet necessary decision, a part of Charlotte's plan to push herself forward and create a new life. The yard sale and throwing-out of old possessions had nearly destroyed her, but decorating the new place with antiques and fresh design had thrilled her, captivating her during the darker and slower winter months.

Sometimes, she caught herself thinking that this was the home where she and Everett would grow old. But often, she shoved those thoughts away. She'd thought the same thing about the old house and Jason. You just couldn't count on anything in this life and had to appreciate the here and now. She knew that (no matter how much it broke her heart to remember it).

"Who's on the porch?" Rachel asked as Charlotte stopped the engine.

Charlotte's eyes became slits. Sure enough, four figures sat around the porch table. A candle flickered between them. Through the silence of the night, there came the crackle of a stereo.

"Seems like we found ourselves a little party," Charlotte said.

Rachel and Charlotte limped up the driveway, overwhelmed with exhaustion. Two of the figures popped up and squealed, "Rach!"

"Gail? Abby?" Rachel dug into her teenage energy sources and rushed forward, hugging her cousins and best friends tightly. "You won't believe this crazy wedding we just did."

Everett and Claire showed their faces after that, wrapping their arms around Charlotte and guiding her to a porch chair. Someone handed Charlotte a glass of wine; another handed her a homemade chocolate chip cookie. Her legs shook with exhaustion, but a contented smile played out across her lips. This was home.

"We've been dying to know what happened today," Everett began, his eyes flickering with the light from the candle.

"Yeah! What did Felicity do?" Claire asked conspiratorially. "Did she storm into the kitchen and scream at the chef?"

"Did she scream at the groom for messing up his vows?" Abby guessed.

"Did she tear apart all the flowers?" Gail asked.

"Gosh, I hope not!" Claire cried. Her eyes became cartoonishly big.

"Actually," Charlotte began, taking a sip of her wine. "Everything started out really well."

"It was eerie," Rachel piped up. "Like Felicity had become an angel. She was laughing with her bridesmaids and even sometimes getting along with her mom."

"When she said her vows, I actually believed them!" Charlotte exclaimed.

"You said before that Felicity and Harvey were doomed for a life of misery?" Everett said.

Charlotte laughed. "Well, let's see. What happened next, Rach?"

"The bride was dancing and having a grand old time," Rachel continued. "But then, disaster struck."

"She tore her dress!" Charlotte cried. "And just at that moment, I'd wheeled out the cake."

"The cake Christine made?" Claire asked.

"That very one. And she immediately screamed at me, telling me it was the wrong cake and that she'd chosen another one. Blah blah. I thought I was going insane. I mean, the number of conversations I had with that horrible girl about cakes... You wouldn't believe it."

Everett stuck a hand up and wore a cheeky smile.

"Actually, I can attest that I heard at least three hours of conversations about said cakes."

"Yeah. Everett deserves an award for getting us through this wedding," Charlotte affirmed. "But really, the groom saved the day."

Abby, Claire, and Gail all leaned forward, captivated. Only Everett seemed to care just the slightest. He was a man, after all. Wedding drama simply hadn't been made for his kind.

"He shoved cake into her mouth!" Rachel exclaimed. "And basically, told her to shut up."

"Then, she shoved cake in his mouth, and we all got back to the party," Charlotte affirmed. "It was a sight to be seen. I can tell you that. But the rest of the reception went on without a hitch."

Everett lifted his beer can. It twinkled in the candle-light. "Let's make a toast to Felicity and whoever is trapped with her for all eternity!"

Charlotte cackled, tossing her head back. Everett's firm hand found her knee, steadying her. Another wave of exhaustion took hold as Rachel began to describe another bit of chaos at the wedding. Slowly, Charlotte dropped her head onto Everett's chest and listened to the steady pounding of his heart.

Not long after, the three teenage girls became conspiratorial, whispering together. Claire wagged her eyebrows and said, "Uh oh. What are they scheming?"

But, just as ever, they just wanted a sleepover. There was something so unique about the "teenage girl sleep-over," something that couldn't be recreated in later years. Sometimes, Charlotte was allowed a glimpse into that world and sat with Abby, Gail, and Rachel, eating snacks and gossiping about all things high school. But more often, she recognized that they had to "let" her in. She wasn't always welcome.

"Come on back to our place," Claire said to Rachel firmly. "You know that you're always welcome."

Charlotte's yawn said everything she needed to say. Claire laughed and hugged Charlotte, whispering, "I'll let her sleep in and feed her breakfast. I'll check in with you tomorrow?"

"You're a lifesaver," Charlotte told her, her mouth slowly closing after the massive yawn.

Everett and Charlotte remained silent, watching as Claire, Rachel, Gail, and Abby walked back to Claire's place. The walk was no more than a quarter of a mile and had been part of the reason that Charlotte and Everett had selected this home in the first place. Charlotte's heart swelled with love as she burrowed herself deeper against his chest, falling into his armpit.

Everyone she loved in the world was close and within her reach.

Well, everyone except Jason— but in truth, she often felt Jason all around her, in the island air and in Rachel's smile.

"You've done it again, Montgomery," Everett teased her, drawing her out of her reverie. "You've managed to pull off an impossible wedding."

"Thanks. Another one down."

Everett dropped his head over hers. They were cocooned together, watching the day fade toward midnight.

"I just got a pretty cool call," Everett said suddenly.

"Yeah?" The excitement tinged in Everett's voice brought Charlotte's head back up. "What's up?"

"*National Geographic* wants me to write a piece about Orcas Island," he continued.

Charlotte's mouth parted in surprise. Since they'd met, Everett had worked tirelessly to get out of the "events photography" game and into something more substantial. Namely: he wanted to merge writing with his love of photography. It was clearly paying off.

"You love that island," she stammered.

"I know! And it's so close to my family in Seattle," he continued.

"What's the story?"

"It's about local life on the island," Everett explained. "And I asked a restaurateur for an interview about his place. He's owned it for thirty-five years. It's a staple."

Charlotte's eyes watered with a mix of fatigue and excitement. "When are you off?"

"Sometime in the next week," Everett explained. He then slipped his fingers through hers. "And I would really love it if you came with me."

Charlotte began to protest. But already, Everett sensed her alarm and said, "Wait. Hear me out. You don't have another wedding for another two weeks. I know because I checked the calendar."

"Yeah. That's true."

"And Rachel doesn't start her senior year until August 18th," Everett continued.

"Yeah..."

"And when she starts her senior year, you're going to be full-speed ahead with senior activities and also autumn weddings," Everett said. "So actually, right now is the only time we could go. Just us."

Charlotte pressed her lips together, her heart surging with love. This handsome man— who just happened to be in love with her— wanted to take her on a beautiful vacation to an island in the northwest. *This wasn't the kind of thing you were legally allowed to say "no" to. Right?*

"I'll just have to ask Claire if she can watch Rachel," Charlotte told him tentatively.

Everett waved a hand. "I wanted to ask her so badly tonight. But I knew it had to come from you."

Charlotte couldn't have put into words just how much that meant to her, the fact that he understood that Rachel's life was up to Charlotte and up to Charlotte alone. When Charlotte entered into this relationship with Everett, she hadn't done it to give Rachel a "new dad." Everett respected this difference; he saw the boundary, and he never crossed it.

It made her love him that much more.

And she told him, now, as the stars illuminated over the Vineyard Sound and as the rest of Oak Bluffs slept. "I love you, Everett. I love you so much."

Chapter Four

The alarm clock on the bedside table blared at half-past five. Wes Sheridan opened his eyes to a brand-new day, watching as the tree limbs swayed gently out the bedroom window and the first of the soft morning light crept across the Sheridan House. Now that Wes was sixty-nine years old (how was that possible?), it often felt as though every bone ached.

Wes swung his legs off the bed and placed the ends of his toes on the ground. For the hundredth time, he asked himself where in the heck he was. In an instant, it flooded back: he was in the newly-built downstairs of the Sheridan House— bedrooms that Scott Frampton had graciously built. With everyone back on the island after so many years away, they'd needed the space.

Gosh, after so many years of heartache and loneliness, Wes often laughed at the sheer number of Sheridan relatives underfoot these days. Max was now hustling around, a toddler of a year and a half with a real penchant for trouble. Christine's baby, Mia, was as cute as a button, peering out from her carrier with earnest, blue eyes.

Audrey and Amanda scrambled in and out of the house, often with their boyfriends. And now, Christine, Lola, and Susan all had partners of their own— Christine being the only one not married yet.

For decades, Wes Sheridan had thought his luck had run out. Boy, he'd been wrong. But wasn't it a curse that the luck began again only after he was diagnosed with early-onset dementia? He wanted to remember each moment of his life with these important people, his family. But how?

The diaries had helped. In fact, since he'd taken to writing nearly everything down, the world had offered him more clarity. He remembered what he'd done, who he saw, who'd said what, and what his plans for the week were. If he didn't quite remember something, he could trust that he'd written something about it already in his diary.

Since he'd started the diary process, he'd filled nearly three diaries. He stacked the others proudly on his desk. Even though they were probably ordinary-sized books, they felt thick to him. They were detailed entries of his life.

That morning, however, didn't necessitate a peek into one of these diaries. He knew why he'd set his alarm early.

Wes donned a flannel top and a pair of pajama pants, then opened the door between his bedroom and the kitchen. Next to his bedroom, Amanda's bedroom door remained closed. This was a funny thing, as Amanda was normally the first one up in the morning. Often, she had oatmeal and coffee prepped and ready for him and Audrey. "We all need to eat more brain food," Amanda said so often, eyeing Wes knowingly.

Wes sometimes wanted to tell his granddaughter that a few grains of oatmeal probably wouldn't reverse the symptoms of his dementia. But he also knew she needed hope, in some way. He had to let her have that.

Wes showered and combed his gray hair, using the reflection in the foggy mirror to assist him. Upstairs, Max let out a single cry and then seemed to put himself back to sleep. Wes laughed to himself, filling with love for that little guy. He'd had quite a difficult start in the world. During his weeks at the NICU, Wes had written every day about Max's bettering health. Wes didn't like to read those diary entries very much— but he was glad he had them. Maybe one day, Max would like to read them.

Wes stepped out on the back porch and stretched his arms toward the sky. His arms creaked ominously but then felt light, limber. Soft light played out across the Vineyard Sound, illuminating the coastal rocks and reflecting off the bright green leaves.

And there, seated in the swing down by the dock, sat Beatrice.

His heart thudded with longing. He wrapped his hands around the scratchy wood of the railing and dared himself to play it cool. As he headed toward the waterline, Beatrice turned to catch his eye. She shared a smile and lifted her binoculars to her eyes, watching as he got closer and closer.

Wes matched her, placing his binoculars over his eyes. He stopped for a moment and peered at everything that was her— the gray hairs that swirled with the sea breezes and the crinkling laugh lines around her eyes. Wes dropped the binoculars and said, "I hope those binoculars aren't showing you any of my faults?"

To this, Beatrice replied, "What faults?"

"Don't you dare flatter me," Wes shot back, his belly bouncing with laughter.

Beatrice placed her finger to her lips while her eyes danced with excitement. Wes had forgotten himself and spoken too loudly, and already, three birds fled the first line of trees and embarked out across the Vineyard Sound. Wes and Beatrice watched, captivated. Very soon, the birds became two black dots, hovering over the rolling ocean.

Wes reached the waterline and stood about a foot to Beatrice's left. The silence felt pregnant. Wes, so inexperienced in the world of love after so many years away from it, held his tongue, terrified he would say the wrong thing.

But after another long and beautiful pause, Beatrice rubbed her elbow into his upper arm playfully and whispered, "That sight makes it all worth it."

The sunrise streaked the glorious waves with orange and yellow hues. To their right, a bird squawked expectantly, as though all the birds in the nearby wooded area awaited Wes and Beatrice.

It was time for them to go.

They walked softly, toe to heel, as they eased through the light between the trees. Wes, who normally lost himself in the mystery of searching for birds along the waterline, caught himself eyeing Beatrice instead. She walked so delicately, like a ballerina. He wondered if she'd ever danced before or if she'd studied it as a teenager. He'd danced with her at Tommy and Lola's wedding— an event that had thrilled him (and, naturally, made his daughters gossip themselves to bits). In his arms, Beatrice had been smooth and delicate. He'd told himself that he would never be enough.

But was it possible? Could they build a second chance?
Or was he kidding himself?

Suddenly, Beatrice's hiss penetrated Wes's thoughts. She pointed toward the waterline, where a crane stretched its long, strong neck and lifted its beak. It was remarkable, almost like a dinosaur, its feathers catching the light and turning almost silver. Wes pressed his binoculars to his eyes as his heart thudded and slowed. Often, when he gazed at nature like this, his body loosened and became gentle. It was as though he was reminded that he, too, would one day return to nature— that, in fact, he already was a part of nature. Most humans forgot that.

Beatrice and Wes crept through the woods for a good hour with their binoculars lifted as birds twittered and danced around treetops. When the sun burned higher in the morning sky, they reached the edge of the property on the far end of Scott and Susan's new house. Wes's legs screamed and demanded that he pause for a moment and lean against a tree. Beatrice rubbed the tops of her thighs with her fist and whispered, "It's really something, isn't it?"

Wes, who could hardly believe his luck, could only nod.

"But I have to admit that I'm getting kind of tired. And hungry," Beatrice added.

Wes's smile jumped across his face. In a whisper, he said, "I'm glad I don't have to be the first to admit it. I'm famished, too."

Wes and Beatrice wandered up to the edge of Scott and Susan's. Inside the house, an orange lamp burned in the kitchen as Susan prepared for the day ahead. On the second floor, Kellan (Wes's normal birdwatching companion) slept, his light still dark. Very soon, Kellan would head off to college at the University of Massachusetts, his major undecided. Wes had told him several times not to worry himself about what he wanted to do. *"Life finds a way of telling you what you'll become,"* Wes had told him.

He hoped that Kellan took that sentiment to heart.

When they reached the trail closer to the road, Beatrice exhaled and tossed her head back as she removed the band around her gray hair. Her motions were upbeat and girlish, and her hair bounced like a shampoo commercial.

"That was gorgeous, Wes," she told him. "I don't know how I got so lucky."

Wes laughed. "I've asked myself the same thing every day of my life."

"Goodness. The idea of growing up here!" Beatrice removed a small container of lotion from her purse and squelched some lavender-scented cream across her hand.

Lavender. *It had been Anna's favorite scent.* Wes closed his eyes as powerful memories swarmed his brain. *Anna, her lotion, her shampoo, and nearly every room of their home— it had all been lavender.*

"Wes? Are you all right?" Beatrice's hand crept across Wes's lower arm. Wes opened his eyes to find her gorgeous blue ones peering back. She seemed to stare into his soul.

"I'm just fine," he told her. His voice wavered, proof that he really wasn't. "I just need something to eat."

They arrived at the Sunrise Cove Inn and entered the front door. This was an act Wes had performed perhaps one million times. Now, he entered as a "visitor," he supposed, rather than the owner and manager and all-around "everything" man. The idea of transferring that power off to his children had terrified him. But when he'd nearly burned down his house (gosh, had that really happened?), he'd known it was time.

"Mr. Sheridan! How are you doing this beautiful morning?" Sam, the front-desk manager who Susan had hired the previous year, stepped around the front desk and shook his hand. He was confident in the way all twenty-something men are confident, yet with the added benefit of actually knowing what he was doing. You believed in him. Wes was glad for that.

"Just fine, Sam." Wes shook Sam's hand. "I woke up before your fiancée this morning if you can believe it."

Sam laughed. "That won't sit well with Amanda. She likes to be first."

"Don't I know it." Wes winked, his heart brimming. "And I'm sure you remember my friend, Beatrice?"

"Oh yes. How could I forget?" Sam had been involved in the hit-and-run accident that had left Beatrice wheel-chair-bound during her first weeks on the island. "How are you feeling, Beatrice?"

"Oh, right as rain." Beatrice's smile blanketed any anxiety she now felt about the accident. She then told him about several of the birds she and Wes had witnessed out along the waterline before waving a hand and saying, "Oh, but I'm blabbering. It's because we're just about starved. Wes? Where is that beautiful Bistro of yours?"

Wes and Beatrice sat at the corner table in the back of the Bistro, the one along the bay window with the near-perfect view of the docks. There, fifty-plus sailboats creaked along the docks, their sails coiled tightly. It looked like they were sleeping.

A server arrived to take their order. Beatrice ordered Eggs Benedict and a cup of coffee. Wes considered oatmeal, remembering Amanda's orders for "more brain food." In the end, though, he opted for bacon, eggs, and biscuits. As he passed the menu back to the server, he told Beatrice, "Maybe it isn't so good for my health."

"But it's good for your spirit," Beatrice told him.

Wes was taken aback. His emotions rolled through him like an approaching storm along the water. He had the strangest itch to place his hand over Beatrice's tiny one, there on the table. But why on earth would she ever want to deal with the likes of him? He was broken on the inside and on the outside, while Beatrice had a long life ahead of her. She was a naturopathy doctor, after all.

Wes had read something on the internet about "Dating After Sixty." He'd felt silly typing that onto Audrey's computer (and hoped that she'd never learned that he'd done that). The site had reminded him to ask numerous questions about the person he was interested in. "People so often forget to give other people space to talk."

So, just after the server arrived back with two mugs of coffee, Wes heard himself ask, "Tell me. How is it going at the Katama Lodge?"

Beatrice perked up after that. She sipped her coffee and jabbered about her new colleagues, Janine Grimson and Nancy, Carmella, and Elsa Remington. "Carmella and Elsa are sisters and just about as different as can be," Beatrice explained. "But according to Janine, their step-sister— Carmella and Elsa recently found common ground. They lost so much over the years. First, their brother, then their mother. After that, a stepmother did her best to put a wedge between them. You can still feel the cracks in their relationship; they're only human, after all. But goodness, I've fallen in love with that team."

"Martha's Vineyard is nothing but good folks," Wes

tried. A split-second later, however, his stomach curdled with the memory that Stan Ellis— the man Anna had had an affair with all those years ago— was friendly with the women of the Katama Lodge. As Hurricane Janine had torn across Martha's Vineyard the previous autumn, Stan had scooped up the Remington women and taken them to safety.

But that was a topic for another time.

"Dad? What are you doing here?" Christine breezed across the Bistro, untying her flour-stained apron. Slight bags hung under her eyes, a reminder that, alongside her busy baking schedule at the Bistro, she also had a baby at home.

"I was out birdwatching and had a craving for your homemade biscuits," Wes replied as he stood on creaking legs and hugged his middle daughter. "You know me, honey. I always think with my stomach."

Christine chuckled. "I'd be worried if you didn't." As their hug broke, she lifted a hand in greeting to Beatrice and said, "By the look of those binoculars, I take it you were out there birdwatching, as well?"

"That's right," Beatrice said proudly. "Your father told me Kellan isn't so eager to wake up in the mornings these days. I'm playing substitute."

"The fact that my father got a teenage boy interested in birdwatching in the first place is incredible, in and of itself," Christine added, her smile stretching into a big yawn. "Gosh, I'm sorry. I really have to hit the road. Zach needs to come in soon to start prep for the day."

"Your turn to watch that darling great-granddaughter of mine?"

"That's right," Christine said, tilting her head adoringly. "She's getting so big. She's growing out of her six-month clothes and breaking my heart along with it."

This version of Christine— at forty-three years old, was night and day from the teenage version, who'd kept to her bedroom and played loud and aggravating music. The change was a welcome one, even if it continued to mystify Wes.

* * *

After breakfast, Beatrice tapped her napkin delicately around her lips and lifted her eyes to Wes's. Her plate shone with yellow yolk, and she told him that she "couldn't possibly eat another bite."

"Me neither," Wes admitted, although when he glanced down, he realized he'd nearly scraped his plate clean. He laughed at himself, and Beverly joined him.

"I had better head up to Katama," she said. "Work awaits me!"

Wes stood slowly to walk her out. He crept along, chatting amicably with her until they reached the door. There, she surprised him by placing her lips against his cheek and then removing them, quick as a flash. It was almost like they hadn't been there at all.

"Thank you for the gorgeous morning, Wesley," Beatrice breathed. "I hope to see you soon."

Wes tried to hold the events of that morning in his head. He had his diary in his bag, and he planned to write down everything he could in it— what she'd said, what he'd told her, what they'd eaten, and everything in between. He wandered, light as air, back to the foyer, where he discovered Amanda and Sam. Sam leaned over the front desk and cradled Amanda's hands in his as she talked to him about something. They looked perfect, young lovers on the precipice of the rest of their lives.

What seemed like a split-second later, Wes found himself behind the desk of the main office in the Sunrise Cove. He had his diary in front of him and his pen lifted. A strange voice in the back of his head told him it was "time to work." But another voice obliterated that, reminding him, *"You aren't in charge of the Sunrise Cove anymore. You're an old man. Anna is dead."*

He inhaled sharply and dropped his shoulders. And then, his heart steadying along, he placed his pen to the diary and began to write. Whatever he remembered that morning would remain sacred, forever.

Chapter Five

"This is it, Mom. This is the dress." Rachel stood in Charlotte's walk-in closet with an emerald dress lifted to her slight frame. Behind it, Rachel stood in shorts and a tank top, her toenails painted lime green.

Charlotte inspected the dress— it was made with satin fabric and had a high neck, with buttons up the back. "It's beautiful. I'd forgotten about it. But what do you mean, anyway? What 'dress' are you talking about?"

Rachel rolled her eyes effortlessly into the back of her head, trained in the art of making her mother feel like a fool. "Mom, come on. This is your and Everett's big, romantic trip away. You've been dating for almost two years, and he literally lives with us. You do the math."

Charlotte waved a hand and turned her attention back to her wide-open suitcase, which she'd only half-filled since she'd begun to pack a half-hour ago. "Everett is going to Orcas Island for work. I'm just tagging along."

"No reason the trip can't mean more than one thing," Rachel grumbled as she spread the green dress across the king-sized mattress. "Pack it. You might need it. That's all I'm saying."

Charlotte poked her tongue into the side of her mouth, making her cheek bulge. Rachel trudged back to the walk-in closet, shifting her hips around to the beat of the music on the stereo. Charlotte was eternally grateful to her teenage child because she constantly knew what was "in" within the world of music— and what was "out." (Not that she always played by Rachel's rules.)

You do the math. The words rang through Charlotte's ears. Naturally, she'd considered the possibility of this. You'd have to be an idiot not to. Perhaps Rachel now thought Charlotte was.

"But if it happens..." Charlotte began, her nostrils flared. *What was she saying?*

Rachel gripped the doorframe and shot her mother a "look."

"You know. If it does..." Charlotte sounded hesitant.

"If you think I'd be anything but over the moon for you, you're crazier than I thought," Rachel shot back.

With careful precision, Charlotte folded the emerald dress and placed it delicately in the suitcase. Immediately, she dared herself to dream of those foggy blue islands along the northwestern coast— dared to imagine that Everett would drop down on one knee and whisper the words she never imagined she'd hear again. "Will you marry me?"

And in these dreamy images, Charlotte allowed herself to picture this particular emerald dress. Rachel was right. It was perfect.

* * *

39

Gail yanked open the front door and yelped back to her twin. "Rachel's here!" Charlotte stepped back as Gail tossed herself into Rachel's arms and jabbered, already, about something Rachel "just had to see." Abby danced forward, wearing a crop top and a pair of short shorts. Charlotte so often wished she could tell her daughter and her nieces to hold off on that kind of clothing. *They only had so much time to be young; why did they push toward adulthood with such force?*

"No hello for your Aunt Charlotte?" Charlotte stepped into Claire's foyer and laughed as the girls scampered up the staircase.

"Hello, Aunt Charlotte!" Gail and Abby called in unison.

Claire stepped out of the kitchen with a bottle of wine lifted. "Care for an afternoon pick-me-up before you head off the island?"

Claire's smile was the most nourishing thing Charlotte knew. In the kitchen, she watched as her sister poured her a glass before returning the bottle of rosé to the fridge. Claire then lifted her glass mischievously and said, "Here's to your big trip away. Wonder what will happen?"

Charlotte swatted Claire gently. "You and Rachel won't give me a break."

Claire cackled. "That daughter of yours has a good head on her shoulders."

Upstairs, a roar of laughter came from one of the girls' bedrooms. Claire and Charlotte lifted their chins and laughed to themselves until they quieted.

"What are they up to up there?" Charlotte asked.

"I'm too scared to ask," Claire replied. "They're seventeen now. I have to assume they're up to no good."

"And next year? We won't have any say in what they do," Charlotte agreed, wrinkling her nose.

Claire clucked her tongue. "Seniors! Where did the time go?"

"No idea. I blinked, and everything changed."

It wasn't entirely true. There had been a whole lot of "stories" between now and Rachel's birth— and a whole lot of tragedy, too. Still, Charlotte ached to cling to these final moments with her only child. She wasn't sure she could ever let go.

"But seriously," Claire began again. "If he asked you, would you say yes?"

"Asked me what?" Charlotte asked, feigning ignorance.

"You're mean," Claire teased.

"And you're nosy."

Rachel fled down the staircase to say a final goodbye to her mother. Already, she smelled like overwhelming perfume and had tried on what looked to be glitter lipstick. Rachel burrowed her face into her mother's shoulder. "Send me pictures. Don't post anything stupid on social media. I love you."

Charlotte guffawed playfully. "I would never post anything stupid on social media."

Rachel's smile was electric. "We'll have to see, won't we?"

Charlotte hugged her sister next. "Thanks for doing this."

"It's no trouble at all. They're just going to be upstairs, giggling, until you get back next week," Claire told her.

"I know." Charlotte stepped back and swatted the

back of her neck. Guilt rolled over her. Already, Rachel scampered upstairs to rejoin her cousins.

"And you said it already. You'll be back two days before her first day of senior year," Claire reminded Charlotte. "You'll have plenty of time to make senior memories. Plus, we'll have a whole year of teenage arguments and silly memories and prom dress shopping. You'll only be grateful you took this trip. Mark my words."

Charlotte squeezed Claire's shoulder gently. In a whisper, she said, "I don't know what I would do without you."

Claire, ever silly, winked and said, "Don't I know it." She then added, "Love you, sis. Text me when you get to Orcas Island. And I, for one, hope you post plenty of stupid stuff on social media. The more, the merrier."

"Hilarious!" Charlotte dropped into the steam of the August afternoon, lifted a hand in final greeting, and called out, "I love you!" She then directed herself back toward home, where Everett awaited her— anxious to hit the road.

Chapter Six

The Pacific Northwest's Orcas Island was the largest island in the San Juan region, an archipelago of gorgeous rocky coastlines and dense emerald forests. Already, it seemed too good to be true.

According to Charlotte's research, Orcas Island itself was aptly named, with many visitors and locals alike spotting orca whales playing in the ocean. Harbor seals and porpoises swam past like a sort of daydream while bald eagles and falcons circled overhead. The island itself was shaped like an M, as though God himself had wanted to carve more shoreline from an already gorgeous piece of the world.

But it was one thing to read about Orcas Island and still another to see it with her own eyes.

When Charlotte and Everett arrived, the Pacific Northwest had kicked up a subtle rain. It tapped gently across their rental vehicle as they drove slowly off the ferry. Charlotte waved to the dockworker, remembering Vineyard rules. She always said hello. She'd raised Rachel to do the same. Lucky for Charlotte, this island seemed to operate with the same rules. The dockworker, dressed in a shiny raincoat, lifted a hand and waved, a smile spreading between his chunky cheeks.

The magazine had booked Everett and Charlotte a room at the downtown Harbor Inn, a quaint little place in a restored Victorian home. According to the plaque outside, the house itself had been built in the late 1800s, not long after the first European settlers had arrived. Another plaque said that the island honored its Native American roots, with tribes inhabiting the gorgeous island beginning about thirteen thousand years ago. Charlotte whistled and pointed. "Now that's an article, Everett. Thirteen thousand years of history!"

Inside the Harbor Inn, a woman in her fifties with an authoritative friendliness (not unlike Susan's) greeted them and handed them their large iron key.

"I hope you two brought your rain gear!" she chirped pleasantly. "Out on Martha's Vineyard, I know you enjoy blissful blue skies most days. But out here in the Pacific Northwest? We embrace the rain. It's part of our soul."

Charlotte assured her that she'd packed not only a raincoat but rain boots, too. "I couldn't resist buying new ones," she admitted. "My daughter told me to seize the opportunity for some new fashion."

The Susan-like woman chortled, as though the idea of having "fashionable" rain boots was foreign to her. Charlotte couldn't blame her. She probably sounded ridiculous.

Charlotte and Everett's suite was located on the top floor of the Victorian house. The ceilings were slanted so dramatically that Everett had to bend low in some parts of the room to avoid hitting his head. Charlotte bounced at the edge of the creaking bed, watching as he scouted his way across the room to the bathroom.

"Be careful out there, explorer," she teased him.

Everett hovered in the doorway between the bathroom and the rest of the suite, puffing out his chest playfully. "Me? Careful? I don't know the meaning of the word!"

With Everett in the bathroom, Charlotte allowed herself to fall into a cavern of silence. A tiny voice in the back of her head demanded: *What if this is it? What if he's the one— the next one, the ticket out of the biggest and loneliest sorrow of your life? What if you're allowed to laugh like this the rest of your life (or at least however long you're allowed to be on this earth together)?*

The door creaked open to reveal Everett wearing a goofy grin. He stood in a black button-up and only his boxers, and his long legs stuck out, muscular and covered with coarse hair.

Charlotte leaped to her feet and cried, "Help! Big Foot! He's real! Help!"

Everett ripped across the room and tackled her across the bed. Her shrieks echoed from one end of the room to the next and probably rushed down the stairwell.

Through giggles, Charlotte said, "That woman downstairs is going to come up here and yell at us!"

"Are you scared of the innkeeper?" Everett teased her.

Charlotte nodded ever-so-slightly.

"You are?" Everett gasped. "Wow. I thought you were braver than that, Charlotte Montgomery."

"Well, maybe I'm not. Maybe I'm a wimp," Charlotte quipped. "What are you going to do about that?"

Everett shook his head, feigning disappointment.

After that, he closed the distance between their lips. With her eyes closed, Charlotte was only aware of his warm body on hers, his soft lips, and the padding of the rain across the windowpanes. It was heaven.

Martha's Vineyard was over three thousand miles away. But just then, it was almost as though it didn't exist.

They freshened up. Charlotte found herself in the bathroom, slipping that emerald dress over her shoulders and cursing her own reflection. Rachel was right: she looked dang good in that dress. It was the sort of dress you wanted to get engaged in. Was she jinxing herself if she put it on now? Was she actually that superstitious?

Downstairs, Everett unfurled a black umbrella to catch the rain. His dark eyes seemed to go everywhere at once, taking stock of the beautiful downtown. On either side of them, houses, restaurants, and bars touted sharp, red rooves, which pointed toward the cloudy sky. Above them, forests roamed across the hills, dense and probably filled with bears and other terrifying wildlife. Charlotte laced her arm around Everett's and tugged him closer to her. He then bent down to kiss her forehead adoringly.

"There it is." They stood in front of a shack with a low-hanging sign that read: JEFF'S.

"It looks like a pit stop on your way someplace else," Charlotte whispered.

Everett nodded. "That's the beauty of it. It's supposed to be one of the best restaurants across the west coast."

"I'll believe it when I see it," Charlotte teased.

* * *

Inside the shack, a mahogany bar stretched from one end of the large room to the other. Charlotte was reminded of old log cabins. On the far wall, an entire bear skin hung, its mouth opened into a "growl." Portraits of cowboys and Native Americans lined the walls, painted with tans and browns and blacks. It made the room gloomy and dark.

Only a few people sat at the bar. They were all men in their fifties or sixties, nursing what was probably their fifth or sixth beer. Charlotte lifted a hand in greeting, but none of them waved back. Apparently, they hadn't heard of island rules.

One of the men at the bar sniffed at them. "You aren't from around here."

Everett loosened his grip on Charlotte. "Actually, I grew up in Washington."

"But not on Orcas Island."

Everett's smile was crooked and utterly handsome. Charlotte thought he could charm the pants off of anyone. *Apparently, not these folks.*

"You have me there," Everett told him. He then cleared his throat and added, "I'm here to meet with Jeff, actually." He tapped his camera case as he added, "I'm here to take some photos and do a brief interview."

"We don't need publicity here," another guy at the bar spat, massaging his pint glass.

Just then, the double doors at the back of the restaurant pushed open to reveal a burly mountain man in a vest and a pair of stained jeans. Across his chest and lap, he wore an apron, which also seemed stained from sauces and meat. He brooded behind that beard of his, which Charlotte was grateful to see he'd wrapped with a hairnet. *Apparently, hygiene still existed in a place like this.*

"This man here is from the city. Says he's here to take photographs," one of the men at the bar tattled on them.

"You got a problem with that, Hank?" Jeff demanded as his nostrils flared.

It was obvious that he was the sort of man who could take down a bear with a single shot. That bear on the wall was proof. Charlotte wondered if he'd made something of the bear's meat. Surely somewhere, they ate things like bear. She shivered.

Everett sweet-talked his way through the next few minutes, discussing his aim for the article and his wish to uphold the unique qualities of Jeff's place. Jeff grunted along, then nodded and crossed his arms as he stood, sturdy and strong, at the other end of the bar.

"That's actually perfect," Everett said as he waved his hand toward him. "Don't move a muscle."

"You're telling him not to move? He'll knock your socks off," another guy at the bar said.

But Jeff did as he was told. He stood like stone as Everett took several photographs of him, both within the context of his restaurant and close-up shots. When he was finished, Everett made a soft noise in the base of his throat. Charlotte knew that noise well— it meant he was pleased with his work.

After that, Jeff disappeared into the kitchen and returned with a feast. Most dishes were meat or fish-based, like perfectly seasoned bison burgers, clams, fish and chips, prosciutto-wrapped oysters, salmon, and steak. He'd portioned out the dishes just so, allowing Everett and Charlotte to experience the flavorings of each plate.

To put it simply: the meat and fish melted off the bone. The seasoning was a revelation, nothing Charlotte had ever experienced before. As she ate, she felt her chin and lips drip with sauces and juices, but she hardly cared at all. It was like she'd fallen into her animalistic impulses.

If only Rachel could see her now.

As Everett ate, he asked Jeff questions, which Jeff could either elaborate on or pass on. It was clear that Jeff did whatever Jeff wanted to do and nothing more. He discussed the thirty-fifth anniversary of opening the restaurant, how he'd built the bar himself, and how he perceived the restaurant industry across the Northwest.

"Orcas Island is a secret we try to keep from the rest of the world," he said under his breath, eyeing Everett as though he wasn't sure he trusted him. "It's important that if it's written about, it's written correctly and accurately. Do you understand?"

Everett nodded that he understood. Charlotte wanted to tell Jeff just how talented Everett was, that he could spin a tale like no man she'd ever met. But she had a hunch that Jeff didn't want to hear a peep out of her. Luckily, there was still a feast before her, keeping her mouth occupied. She had no room to speak.

After dinner, Jeff shook both Everett and Charlotte's hands and led them to the door. Everett explained that the article would be out very soon and that he would contact Jeff immediately. Jeff looked split on the subject. *Did he want publicity? Or did he want to fade into nothingness as his bar eroded around him?*

Outside, Orcas Island had descended to darkness. The air was foggy, lending an almost mystical quality to the downtown streets. Above them, the trees faded into the fog. There were no stars.

"Let's walk to the water," Everett suggested. "I need to walk off that tremendous meal."

Charlotte walked with bated breath. A million ideas

of what to say came to her mind, but she refuted each one. It seemed that Everett had brought her to a mystical world, one that should have only existed in storybooks and films. Perhaps this was all a dream.

They reached the rocky coastline of Madrona Point, where Everett and Charlotte stood on the tip tops of large rocks and peered out as far as they could. On either side of the bay were the jagged edges of Orcas Island.

"There's so much to explore here," Charlotte heard herself breathe. "To think, I know every nook and cranny, every hiking trail, and nearly every resident of Martha's Vineyard, while this place is a mystery."

"Wouldn't it be amazing to get to the bottom of that mystery?" Everett asked. He placed his hand at the base of Charlotte's back and rubbed her aching muscles, a product of the plane seat.

Charlotte laughed. "If only we had more time."

Everett turned his head ever-so-slightly to catch Charlotte's eye. The waves rushed across the stones, filling the jagged space between them. For a long time, they gazed into one another's eyes, captivated. And just before Charlotte thought for sure Everett was about to kiss her, he disappeared.

"Everett!" Charlotte cried.

Everett had slipped and fallen into the puddle of water just below her. Both of his knees bumped the stones, and he tossed his head back, attempting to steady himself. As Everett's laughter echoed out across the water, Charlotte shoved away her terror. She reached down, saying, "Grab my hand! I'll pull you up."

But instead, as he lifted one knee up from the stones, Everett placed a beautiful vintage engagement ring at the end of her fourth finger.

Charlotte's heart thudded so loudly that she couldn't hear the water any longer. She gasped as the ring remained there at the edge of her finger, waiting.

"Charlotte Montgomery..." Everett began.

Charlotte gasped again and began to stagger backward, forgetting that it was rather easy for her to fall as well. Everett rushed to his feet and steadied her, holding her in his arms. One-half of him was soaking wet from his fall.

"Did you really try to get down on one knee and fall in the water?" Charlotte asked, her eyes heavy with tears.

Everett's smile was infectious. "It's a pretty good story, don't you think?"

Charlotte closed her eyes so that a single tear raced down her cheek. During the silence of the moments that followed, it felt as though her and Everett's hearts beat as one.

"I'll marry you," she whispered.

Everett laughed. "I haven't even asked you yet."

Charlotte's eyes popped open in disbelief. But before she could protest, Everett slipped the engagement ring onto her fourth finger and wrapped his arms around her. "Always getting ahead of yourself," he teased her gently, kissing her forehead and the tip of her nose and then, finally, her lips. Charlotte begged herself not to start sobbing; she didn't want to ruin the moment. Everett wrapped his hand tenderly over her cheek and held her, just like that, as the waters of a much different ocean rushed toward them.

The future belonged to them, no matter what island they stood on. Everett had given her the confidence to believe that.

Chapter Seven

News of Charlotte's engagement rushed through the gossip channels of Martha's Vineyard, quick as lightning. The news reached Wes Sheridan only one day after it happened. That afternoon, even as Charlotte and Everett remained an entire continent away, Wes sat on the porch swing overlooking the Vineyard Sound with a glass of iced tea, watching the waves roll across the beach. He was lost in thought, considering the events of the weekend and the haze of memory that so often overwhelmed him as he sat on the back porch. If he shifted his head just so, he could envision Anna on the beach along with their three little girls, making a sandcastle beneath a sky blotchy with clouds.

"Everett popped the question on Orcas Island!" Audrey leaped through the screen door and tore through Wes's reverie.

For a long moment, Wes just blinked at Audrey, his mind foggy. *Everett? Who in the good golly was Everett?* But a split-second later, it came to him. Everett was the handsome photographer who'd fallen in love with his niece, Charlotte, and decided to remain on the island for good. He'd given Charlotte hope in the wake of her husband's death. This— this hope was something Wes had never been allowed after Anna's death. *Until now. Maybe.*

"I'm assuming she told him to hit the road?" Wes asked Audrey mischievously.

"Grandpa," Audrey sighed, feigning exasperation. "You're just not a romantic, are you?"

Amanda appeared behind Audrey, little Max in her arms. She bopped around playfully, her engagement ring catching the light of the late afternoon. "Charlotte got engaged! Charlotte got engaged!" She said it in a singsong voice, making Max giggle madly.

Very soon afterward, Susan plotted an engagement dinner for the following Saturday. She paced up and down the living room of the Sheridan House, clicking a pen as she fantasized about different dinner options for the party. Only Amanda played along with this, acting her part as "Mini-Susan." On the floor at their feet, Audrey built up block towers with Max, who always smacked them back down again.

Exhausted after a long day of walking the beach with Audrey and Amanda, Wes returned to his bedroom, closed the door gently against the sounds of his family's chatter, and lay back on the bed. He then reached over to the bedside table to collect his diary, which he liked to peruse during quiet moments like this. It was good to remind himself of the weekend's events.

He'd met Beatrice again the previous morning to bird-watch and have coffee. He'd asked her numerous questions, many of which he'd remembered to list in the diary immediately after.

He'd written:

Beatrice's Favorite Things: Labrador puppies (she had them growing up), daffodils, bonfires, jet-black squirrels (which she saw on a childhood trip to Michigan), and carrot cake.

Wes read and reread the list, drawing his finger across the words as though they came from a religious text. He then closed the book, placed it back on the bedside table, and slowly drifted to sleep. He didn't dream; his real life felt dreamy enough for him just then.

* * *

That Wednesday, Susan sent out a text message to confirm the date and time of Charlotte's engagement party.

> SUSAN: SATURDAY, AUGUST 20 - Drinks at 6:30 p.m. and Dinner at 8 p.m.

Almost without thinking, Wes grabbed his phone and typed, his thumbs moving as slow as molasses.

> WES: Susan, do you mind if I bring a guest?

A split-second later, a knock rang out on Wes's bedroom door. "Come in," he said.

Audrey appeared in the crack, her smile as mischievous as Max's. She tapped her phone on her thigh and asked, "Do you know that everyone in the group chat can see what you wrote?"

Wes's cheeks burned. They were probably red as cherries. "What are you talking about?"

Audrey lifted her phone to show off the message, which Wes had only just carefully typed. "See? It's a family group chat."

Wes tried to play it cool. "Well, I just figured I could ask."

Audrey's smirk lengthened. "Admit it. You want to ask Beatrice to dinner."

"Audrey..." Wes warned.

"Grandpa! I should have known. All those early-morning birdwatching sessions? I mean, that's the most romantic thing I've ever heard of."

Wes stuttered. "It's not what you think."

Audrey waved a hand just as Wes's phone buzzed with a text message. It was Susan, writing from her personal number and not into the group chat. Obviously, everyone in the family thought he was ill-equipped with technology. And older than dirt.

> SUSAN: Beatrice can come to the party!
> You don't have to ask about that.

Wes groaned and rubbed his palm across his forehead. Audrey giggled and wrapped a hand around Wes's upper arm. Back in the old days, that arm had been heavy with muscle. Wes had been a full-blown "man," whatever that meant. Now, he was just "grandpa."

Had he wasted his life? Oh, what a stupid question. He took a delicate step back toward his bed and locked eyes with Audrey. Audrey's smile faltered.

"Grandpa, you don't need to worry about what anyone thinks," Audrey tried. "We love you. And watching you be happy again is, like, really—"

Behind her, Max tumbled over a pile of blocks. On the ground, he tossed his head up and twisted his face into a howl. Audrey leaped for him and drew him to her chest, whispering, "It's okay, honey. It's okay. You're okay."

Wes disappeared back into his bedroom. Shame hung heavily across his shoulders. He sat at the edge of his bed and blinked down at his toes. He focused on his breathing: *inhale, exhale, inhale, exhale.* It wasn't anything he'd done prior to meeting Beatrice. She'd told him, "*People really discredit the benefits of breathing.*" Was she right? He had no idea.

A little while later, Audrey returned to his bedroom door and knocked at it. Probably, she was eager to apologize for teasing him about the text. Wes, however, was heavy in a text conversation with Beatrice and decided not to answer. He supposed teenagers did this sort of thing all the time.

> BEATRICE: I finally got this phone up and running. Tommy's been a real sport about it.

> BEATRICE: He didn't even call me "old lady" once.

Wes's stomach tightened with anxiety. His thumbs were poised over the screen as a smile played out across his face. *What could he text back?*

> BEATRICE: I hope you're having a good day.

Oh no! He'd waited too long to write her back. She thought he wasn't interested. It was over, long before it had begun. Wes should have known.

He wrote her back, his thumbs fumbling.

> WES: It's been a gorgeous day here. Got word that my niece got engaged over on Orcas Island.

> WES: I can't believe she betrayed us islanders and got engaged on a DIFFERENT island.

> WES: But that's just me.

Was that stupid? Probably. His head hammered with fear. But a split-second later, Beatrice responded. He could practically feel her hovered over her phone, awaiting his response. Had Audrey known about any of this, she would have teased him to no end.

After a good twenty-five minutes of back-and-forth, Wes got up the courage to invite Beatrice to Saturday's engagement party. The second he pressed "SEND," he rocketed to his feet and blinked at the lighted rectangle on his phone, which had suddenly become his entire life.

The text Beatrice sent back meant the world to him. His face split into an enormous smile.

> BEATRICE: I'd love to.

* * *

That Saturday morning, Wes awoke at seven-thirty to discover Amanda on a yoga mat in the living room, her eyes closed and her body in a strange configuration, one that didn't exactly look comfortable. That, apparently, was the point of yoga. Wes trudged into the kitchen and poured himself a mug of coffee as Amanda exhaled all the air from her lungs and placed her palms flat together.

When she opened her eyes, she turned them slowly toward her grandfather as she whispered, "Good morning."

Wes lifted his mug. "You looked like you were really in the zone, there."

Amanda leaped up and rolled her yoga mat into a coil. "I wanted to get in a good session before today's party."

Wes's stomach tightened. He sipped the piping-hot coffee and grimaced. "Did Charlotte and Everett make it back from the west all right?"

"Mom says they made it, which is a good thing. Mom already pre-cooked enough food to feed a small village," Amanda said. She whipped around to put the yoga mat in the back closet, taking her swinging ponytail along with her.

Wes guffawed and wrapped his hand around his neck. "You know, I was thinking."

Amanda swung back around, her eyebrows lifting. "Yeah?"

"I just thought it would be nice to bring something to the party," Wes said.

"What kind of thing?"

"Dessert."

Amanda waved a hand. "Don't worry, Grandpa. Mom cooked enough dessert to feed a second village."

Audrey walked down the staircase, her arms above her head as her massive t-shirt waved around her. "What about dessert?"

"Grandpa wanted to bring dessert tonight," Amanda explained. "But I told him that Mom has it taken care of."

"What's she making?" Wes forced himself to ask.

Amanda lifted her shoulder. "There's lemon bars, a variety of cookies, and ice cream. Maybe something else."

Wes's right hand formed a fist. "I just think it would be nice if we had carrot cake."

Had he actually said that? Did he sound like a whiny person at that moment?

"Oh. Carrot cake! Delicious," Amanda said. "But I really think it's overkill. Maybe next week?" Amanda dropped down to touch her toes, stretching out after her difficult session.

This left Wes to eye the ground. Carrot cake. It had been on the "list" he'd created of things Beatrice liked.

"Why do you want carrot cake so bad, Grandpa?" Audrey asked, her smile crooked and confused.

Wes stuttered, hardly making any sense, even to himself. "Amanda's probably right."

Audrey's eyes widened. She pressed her lips together knowingly and flashed her eyes back and forth. "You know what, Amanda? I think carrot cake sounds really good for tonight."

Amanda arched her eyebrow. "But seriously, Audrey. Mom has so much dessert already."

Audrey rubbed her stomach like a child. "Come on, Amanda. We can't skimp on Charlotte's big party." She yanked her phone from her pocket and clicked around, her eyes dancing. "Here's a recipe for 'The World's Best Carrot Cake.' Grandpa, do you think that'll work for us?"

Wes tried to suppress a smile. He and Audrey locked eyes; the air simmered with understanding and good humor. Only Amanda remained in the dark.

"Whatever," Amanda shot out with a shrug. "Don't pay any attention to that recipe, Audrey. I have a much better one. We'll do it my way."

Within the hour, Audrey, Amanda, and Wes stood at the kitchen counter with their hands washed. The ingredients for Amanda's carrot cake were lined up: robust carrots, sugar, cinnamon, flour, and eggs. Amanda's ponytail continued to flip around with authority. On the ground, Max bobbed around and sang his mother's name. "Mama!"

Amanda put Wes to work. She handed him a wooden spoon and told him to stir the dry ingredients. Throughout, Audrey popped up and down, eager to play with Max and converse with the "adults." Wes sifted through flour and baking soda, his heart pounding against his ribcage. *What on earth was he doing? Was this a proclamation of love?*

"Here. It's time to mix them together." Amanda lifted the bowl of dry ingredients and instructed Wes to "sift" them into the bowl of liquid ingredients. The ingredients snowed down as Wes's wooden spoon struggled through the ever-thickening mixture. The carrots were sharp-looking and orange, very jagged looking against the rest of the dough. Wes prayed that the cake would turn out. He needed this to be delicious. He needed Beatrice to know how much he cared, how much he listened, and, most importantly, how much he remembered.

He remembered, dammit! Even if it was only because of his diary.

Amanda opened the oven and watched dutifully as Wes placed the cake pan on the rack. As he closed it back up again, both Amanda and Audrey howled excitedly. Max clapped his hands along with them, grateful to be involved. Despite his sixty-nine years of life, Wes suddenly felt just as captivated with the baking process as Max probably was. What a remarkable thing.

Wes waited at the edge of the couch cushion, watching his timer as it clicked down to zero. Audrey had the remote control and flicked through the channels, chatting with Amanda, who sat cross-legged on the carpet. Sometimes, Wes had to remind himself that currently, his two roommates were twenty-something women, plus an animated toddler named Max. It wasn't entirely unlike the old days, after Anna's death, when he'd found himself at the mercy of three girls— Lola, age eleven, Christine, age fourteen, and Susan, age seventeen. He hadn't stood a chance.

Audrey settled on a horrendous reality TV show about housewives who seemed to have more money than they knew what to do with. Amanda leaped up from the carpeting to prepare the cake's frosting, which she insisted on doing alone. "You rest, Grandpa." Sometimes, Wes thought Amanda's assumptions of him labeled him too much as an "old man." *He could do things! He was only sixty-nine years old! He planned to live a whole lot more!*

Admittedly, he probably couldn't stir up a frosting quite as good as Amanda's. But that didn't mean he wasn't game to try. He rose from the couch and joined Amanda at the kitchen counter. Amanda held a bag of powdered sugar and arched her eyebrow, eyeing him like he was up to no good. Probably, he wasn't.

"Grandpa? What is this really about?" Amanda finally asked.

Audrey leaped from the couch with more frenetic energy than she should have been allowed. She bounced over to the kitchen and placed her elbows along the counter. "Come on, Amanda. Are you really that dense?"

Amanda's right eyebrow lifted still higher toward her brow line. Wes kept his eyes planted firmly toward the powdered sugar as his cheeks burned hot. Finally, Amanda's lips formed a round O.

"Is this about Beatrice?"

Wes scratched the skin behind his ear. He felt like a little kid, teased at school about the color of his socks or the way he threw a baseball.

"I'm such an idiot," Amanda began.

"No, you're not." Wes's eyes returned to hers. He wouldn't stand for such talk, not from his granddaughter. He could have talked at length about the power of the mind, how the words you told yourself became the words you believed.

Amanda shook her head and handed Wes the big plastic mixing bowl. Her jaw set, she said, "It's a rare thing to find a man who bakes. Beatrice had better hang on to you."

That was all anyone had to say about it.

And within the next hour and a half, the cake was baked, cooled, and frosted. Wes gazed down at the glorious display, a cake that, in his mind, represented his newfound feelings for his newfound friend. He had a drip of icing on his finger, and he licked it, his eyes closed against the creamy sweetness.

"She's going to love it," Audrey whispered, eyeing him from the couch. Max slept against her chest with his long eyelashes draped across his cheeks.

Wes blinked foolishly at her, daring himself to believe in another life. *How could he possibly describe to Audrey how lonely he'd been over the years? How could she possibly understand?*

She hadn't been there. She'd been raised in Boston. Until very recently, the story had gone like this— Wes had been responsible for Anna's death.

And in a way, he was. But not the way his daughters had thought.

Wes splayed the cake across a beautiful cake pan and washed his hands in the sink. Amanda excused herself to shower upstairs as Audrey scuttled off to change Max's diaper. This left Wes in the soft shadows of the kitchen, his hands dripping at his sides and the cake on display on the counter. It was still two hours till Susan's party— and how on earth would he possibly make it? He would count down the minutes with endless expectation. He would ache until he saw Beatrice's gorgeous, bright-blue eyes again.

Chapter Eight

The newly engaged couple sat at the far end of the dining room table. Wes stood clumsily in the doorway, the cake tray across the flat of his palms. Audrey and Amanda rushed off in front of him, attacking Charlotte and Everett with hugs and congratulations. Susan approached, her lipstick perfectly lined over her beautiful lips and her hair styled immaculately. It was often hard to remember that she'd ever had cancer at all.

"Hi, Dad!" Susan placed a hand on the back of Wes's shoulder and kissed his cheek. "What do you have there?"

Wes felt strange, as though his arms and legs were too long for his body. "We brought carrot cake."

Susan blinked twice, clearly confused. It was a rare thing— actually, an unheard-of thing— that Wes Sheridan brought anything like this to the potluck. On cue, Kerry leaped over from the dining room table and hugged Wes, crying out, "Did my brother make something?"

Wes, whose memories of Kerry were burned with

ferocity into the back regions of his mind, laughed good-naturedly. There was nothing Kerry could say to him that would make him feel bad. They'd been through too much together already.

"Is that against the rules?" Wes asked.

Kerry waved a hand. She looked triumphant and joyful, all as a result of Charlotte's new engagement, her new chance at love. *Would Kerry feel the same way about Wes if Beatrice and Wes found a way to make it work? Or would she think he was just a silly old man?*

"Of course not," Kerry replied quickly, trying to set her brother at ease. "I can't wait to try it. Heck, I'll try it even if you poisoned it. Sit down with me, Wes."

Wes allowed Kerry to guide him to the dining room table. As he shifted the chair closer, he eyed Charlotte, his grin widening. "Congratulations, Char!"

Charlotte laughed. "Thank you, Uncle Wes. We're over the moon." She laced her fingers through Everett's. Although she was over forty years old, she looked youthful and vibrant— a woman on the cusp of the rest of her life. It was hard to believe, looking at her, that she'd ever had a moment of hardship.

For so many years, Wes had kept tabs on Charlotte, Claire, and Kelli. He'd ached with jealousy, so angry with himself for having chased his own girls away. Kerry had been allowed to keep her entire family on the island. Admittedly, she'd invited Wes to many events that included dinners, birthday parties, and weddings— anything to make him feel more included. But he'd felt the gaping hole in his own heart, proof that no matter what, nobody could take the place of his own children.

Claire sidled up to Charlotte and wrapped her arms

around her. She then spun around and clapped Everett on the shoulder. "Welcome to the family, Everett."

Everett blushed and locked eyes with Wes for a split second across the table. It was like he sensed how strange Wes felt, watching the chaos unfold before him.

"I can't believe she said yes," Everett told Claire, shifting his gaze toward her. "Spending the rest of your life with this dope? It's a fate worse than death!"

Charlotte swatted him gently and pressed a kiss upon his lips. Wes turned around, his heart fluttering with intrigue. Beatrice had told him she'd be there by six-thirty, which it now was. When he lifted his eyes, he found Audrey with little Max in one arm and a cocktail in her opposite hand. She gave him a mischievous grin.

"What are you up to, Grandpa?" she asked. "Are you plotting and scheming again?"

Noah stepped up to take Max from Audrey. He whirled him around as he squealed with laughter. Wes's heart lifted into his throat.

"I'm not the one around here who plots and schemes," Wes told his granddaughter (the one who, admittedly, was his favorite— a fact he would never admit to anyone).

Audrey grabbed another cocktail from the counter and handed it over to Wes. She bent down and whispered in his ear, "I think I just heard her come through the back door."

Wes sipped the cocktail, something vodka-based that he couldn't register. In all honesty, he couldn't fully register much in those moments. He lifted his chin to eye the far back door, hungry for some proof of what Audrey said.

And a split second later, she emerged from the gray light of the evening.

There stood Beatrice. She eased through the back foyer and removed her high-heeled boots. Her bottle of wine (something she'd brought to be polite) caught the light from the hanging fixture of the small room as she kicked off the last of her shoes. Susan approached, ever ready for a new guest. Susan accepted the wine and commented about it, probably saying whatever it was you were meant to say about wine. Wes hadn't a clue.

Wes drummed up the courage to walk down the hallway to greet Beatrice. As he went, however, Lola rushed up beside him and planted a big kiss on his cheek. She chattered easily, locking him against the wall as she told him about whatever it was she and Tommy had been up to over the previous week. Wes could hardly comprehend what she said. As she talked, Tommy ambled up behind her and greeted his Great Aunt Beatrice, bending down to kiss her cheek and whisper something in her ear. Wes felt the weight of the night slipping through his fingers. Probably, everyone already assumed that Tommy had invited Beatrice to the dinner. Perhaps he actually had!

"You okay, Dad?" Lola stepped back delicately. She traced a strand around her ear and looked vaguely injured, the way she had when she'd gotten her feelings hurt as a girl. Only Wes remembered these sorts of things.

"Wes!" Beatrice somehow carved her way through the masses to greet him. Her eyes were expectant, proof, maybe, that she understood that he'd stumbled into many roadblocks on the way to greeting her. "How are you?"

Wes's smile was effervescent. He longed to wrap his arms around her, to tell her how often she'd entered his mind the past few days. The chaos of the party filled their ears, making it difficult for them to hear.

Finally, Beatrice lifted herself onto her tippy toes to whisper, "You Sheridans and Montgomerys always seem to throw the best parties."

Wes laughed. It was almost a natural laugh. Almost. "I take no credit for any of that."

But suddenly, Susan swung past them, a cocktail lifted. She'd heard what he'd said. "What are you talking about, Dad? You brought a homemade carrot cake. That, alone, makes the party that much better."

At this, Beatrice's eyes widened. She locked eyes with Wes. The memory of many days prior, when she'd confessed her love of carrot cake, sizzled in the air between them. But before Beatrice could speak, Susan called out that another round of drinks had been made and was ready for pick-up on the counter. A line of revelers approached, including Wes's long-time brother-in-law, Trevor. Trevor clapped Wes on the shoulder, shaking him. This broke Wes and Beatrice's eye contact.

"My daughter has found happiness again," Trevor said, his eyes heavy with tears. "What do you think about that?"

How could Wes be anything but thrilled? "It's just incredible."

Trevor dabbed at his cheeks, which were wet with tears. He'd always been emotional, which a sign of strength, at least in Wes's eyes.

Under his breath, Trevor whispered, "When Jason passed, Charlotte became just a shell of who she'd been. It was like looking at a ghost. Now, it's like she's come alive again. It's enough to make me just—" His face scrunched up as his emotions overwhelmed him. Wes, who was an emotional man in his own right, clapped Trevor on the back and grabbed a cocktail from the counter. He pressed it into Trevor's hand and said, "We have to drink to Charlotte's happiness."

Wes and Trevor clinked glasses. Around them, Tommy, Lola, Audrey, Beatrice, Claire, and Kelli brought their glasses in, as well, and hollered, "To Charlotte and Everett!" Wes felt caught up in the pomp and circumstance. He felt like a much younger man.

A few minutes later, Charlotte's eldest brother, Steve, arrived. He strode through the back door, his backpack heavy with bottles of wine and his hands scrubbed clean after his long day at the mechanic shop. He wrapped his powerful arms around his kid-sister and lifted her off her toes as she shrieked. Behind him, his wife, Laura, shook her head and flipped her hair from its ponytail. She swallowed Charlotte in a hug immediately after and said, "We nearly fell on the floor when we heard the news."

Steve and Laura's youngest child, Isabella, followed in after them. At twenty-two, she was slender and anxious, her eyes whipping back and forth to take stock of everyone in the room. Wes hadn't spoken to her often, as she ordinarily kept to herself. But right then, her panic at the sight of so many family members gathered in such a small room was familiar to Wes. He wanted to tell her that he understood her. Probably, that coming from a sixty-nine-year-old man meant very little to someone like her.

"Isabella!" Charlotte cried. "Your father just filled me in on the good news."

Isabella's cheeks burned bright red. She brushed her fingers through her hair and bit her lower lip.

"Don't be bashful, Isabella," Laura told her, drawing

her arm lovingly around her daughter. She lifted her eyes to Charlotte's to add, "It's hard to believe that our baby girl will be leaving the island."

"It's not that I want her to go," Charlotte added. "It's just that I know how talented she is. The world deserves that talent. New York City won't know what to do with itself."

Suddenly, someone squeezed the very end of Wes's elbow. Wes turned around and immediately dropped into the icy blue of Beatrice's glorious eyes.

"You made carrot cake," Beatrice repeated softly. The words were like poetry.

But how could Wes possibly respond? His throat nearly closed. "It's a fantastic dessert," he tried before immediately cursing himself. He felt just like Isabella, put on the spot. "I mean, when you said how much you liked it, I had such an intense craving for it. I knew I needed to make it."

Beatrice's eyes glittered. Wes was reminded of the Vineyard Sound so early in the morning, as the first birds twittered in the soft light.

"Aunt Bea?" Tommy called from the corner. "Would you like an hors d'oeuvres?"

Beatrice seemed to have to drag herself around to face her great-nephew. Wes's heart banged like a drum.

"I'm really all right, Tommy," Beatrice told him. When she turned back, she bent low so that only Wes could hear her. "Sometimes, he pays a little too much attention to me. He thinks I'm such an old lady. I wish I could prove to him that I'm not."

Wes tossed his head back. His laughter filled the room. As everyone was preoccupied with their own conversations, he hardly felt any glances his way.

"I wish I could tell you how much I relate to that," Wes explained as his laughter waned.

Beatrice took a delicate step forward. "Maybe one day, we can tell each other everything. Everything that's on our minds."

Wes's mind seemed to catch fire. *Did she mean what he thought she meant? Or was this all imagined? Was it possible that this "imagination" was a symptom of dementia?*

God, he hoped not.

But before he could properly respond, Susan clinked her fork against her glass and announced that they would soon sit down for dinner. She wore that immaculate smile, the one she donned when she hosted. Toward the far end of the room, Kellan appeared, ruffling his fingers through his hair. His face brightened at the first sign of Wes, and Wes lifted a hand in greeting. Kellan sauntered toward him and wrapped Wes in a hug, telling him excitedly about his first semester of classes. All the while, Beatrice watched Wes like a hawk. It was hard not to think that everything he did was a part of a test. Gosh, he wanted to pass that test so badly. He wanted to prove himself to Beatrice.

He wanted the sort of hope that Charlotte had decided to build her brand-new life upon.

But the night went on without a hitch, with hardly enough drama to write home about. After dinner, dessert was served, and Beatrice ate only carrot cake— licking the tongs of her fork luxuriously and often making eye contact. Wes could have died and gone to heaven.

Had Wes been forty or fifty years younger, he might have asked Beatrice to head home with him for a "night-cap." With an aching heart, he watched as she slipped her light jacket over her shoulder and chatted with Laura about some form of yoga she "swore by" as a naturopath. Laura said, "I'll have to write that down," but she made no motion to do so. Beatrice waved to Wes at the door, and Wes had to suppress every instinct not to leap toward her, hold onto her, and demand that she stay.

It had been ages since he'd felt so drawn to someone.

Yet it seemed eternally difficult to tell if those "urges" were actually real or just the imagination of his lonely heart.

Chapter Nine

It had been the sort of weekend you didn't recover from quickly. Charlotte muddled about in a fog of love, happiness, joy, and "hangover" for the better part of that Sunday, fielding still more "Congratulations!" text messages from loved ones and snuggling with Everett on the couch. Rachel, for better or for worse, spent the majority of the day in her bedroom, watching television.

Her senior year had only just begun. Probably, exhaustion overwhelmed her.

Now, it was the Wednesday after. Rachel had been hard at work on her senior year for the better part of a week, and Charlotte was back in full swing to her wedding planning responsibilities. That afternoon, in fact, she found herself seated at her office desk, on video chat with a client based in Minneapolis, Minnesota. Her wedding would take place on Martha's Vineyard in late spring. Over and over again, she'd informed Charlotte that money "was no object."

That said, Charlotte wasn't entirely pleased about the bride's requests.

"Think *Lord of the Rings* meets *Game of Thrones*," the bride explained over video chat. Her hands burst into little fireworks as she explained. "I want my bridesmaids to be like the elves. And Davey wants his groomsmen to be like the Night Watch. You watched that show, right?"

Charlotte hadn't watched *Game of Thrones*, nor did she remember much about *Lord of the Rings*. If she remembered correctly, she and Jason had made out during one of the films, to the point that a worker at the cinema had told them they had to leave. It was a funny memory, but not one that led her to any images of the movie itself.

"Of course," Charlotte told the bride, playing along. "And the image is really striking."

"Exactly. I want everything to be memorable," the bride continued.

Charlotte's eyes formed slits. In her hand, her pen continued to glide along on a pad of paper, taking notes about the bride's deepest wishes. By the end of their hour-long meeting, Charlotte's eyes were glazed over. She willed herself to tell the bride that she couldn't do it. But when the bride agreed to Charlotte's exorbitant price— Charlotte could do nothing but agree. The pain of this would mean nothing to her once the check cleared.

After she hung up the call, Charlotte exhaled all the air from her lungs, took a sip of tea, and rose up from her office chair. Outside, an August rain landed gently across the back porch. Very soon, the island would lend itself over to the dark shadows of autumn. Very soon, her tank tops and shorts would be stuffed into the containers beneath her and Everett's bed to hibernate until next summer.

Charlotte stepped quietly through the downstairs

hallway and headed for the kitchen. She'd opted for a large bag of peanuts, white chocolate chips, and cranberries during a brief run to the little downtown market, and her cravings had kicked in. These sorts of purchases would be long-gone as soon as she and Everett marked the date of their wedding. Charlotte would be firmly committed to a bride diet. She'd seen it all before.

In the kitchen, Charlotte heard the familiar and soft footfalls of Rachel up on the second floor. With her bag of peanuts poised, Charlotte listened as Rachel paced. There was something amiss about these footfalls. They seemed almost frantic. Charlotte placed a salty peanut on her tongue and chewed slowly. *What was wrong?*

Abandoning the peanuts, Charlotte stepped lightly up the staircase and headed for Rachel's closed bedroom door. She paused outside of it with her knuckles lifted to knock. But a split-second later, Rachel's soft cries crept through the crack beneath the door. Charlotte could have crumpled into a sorrowful ball.

And to her intense shame, Charlotte leaned her ear toward the door to listen. She just had to know what was on her daughter's mind.

"I don't know what to do," Rachel wailed to someone on the phone. "Nobody in third period would even look at me today. That's how bad it was."

Charlotte's stomach twisted. She leaped back, as though the door between herself and her daughter was aflame. Slowly, she stepped back toward the staircase and then hustled back toward the first floor. Rachel's words were burned into her mind. *"Nobody in third period would even look at me."*

Back in the kitchen, Charlotte stuffed white chocolate chips into her mouth and considered her options.

Throughout the previous three years of Rachel's high school life, Charlotte had considered herself very lucky to have a daughter who generally seemed "put together." As far as Charlotte had been able to tell, Rachel was well-liked, with several friends, a good after-school schedule, and very good grades. Even when Jason had passed away, Rachel had gone through high school with flying colors. *What had changed?*

In a flash, Charlotte had Claire on the phone. Claire was her one-stop-shop for all things "what to do about the girls."

"Hi there, blushing bride," Claire answered the phone. In the background, there was the sound of dinner sizzling. Claire often made overly complicated meals that required several hours of cooking. Charlotte wasn't so keen.

"Ha. Hi." Charlotte scrunched her nose. "I don't feel like a blushing bride right now."

"What's wrong?"

Charlotte groaned. "I think I just heard Rachel talking about some drama at school."

"You were eavesdropping?"

"Guilty," Charlotte told her.

"Well. Can't say I blame you. I've eavesdropped a time of two, myself." The sizzling escalated. Claire seemed to bang at something, probably with a spatula, until it calmed down. "What did Rachel say?"

"Something about nobody talking to her in third period? Gosh, it terrified me. We made it three years without any bullying," Charlotte said.

"That you know of," Claire countered.

"Yes. I suppose you're right." Charlotte dropped her

teeth over her lower lip. "Gail and Abby haven't said anything?"

"Not yet," Claire offered. "Should I ask them?"

"No. Gosh, no. I don't want Rachel to know that I eavesdropped on her," Charlotte added. "Just keep tabs on things. Let me know if you hear of anything."

"Will do," Claire told her. "I'm sure it's just senior year jitters. These kids have no idea what to do with their lives, but suddenly, they're being asked really tough questions about their futures. It's alarming."

"It's just as alarming for us," Charlotte told her.

"You got that right."

Charlotte got to work after that. She boiled water, grated too much cheese, made a roux, and watched the pasta bubble and foam in the pot. By the time the homemade macaroni and cheese was steaming and gooey in the pot, it was only four-thirty in the afternoon— far too early for any sort of dinner. Still, if Charlotte knew her daughter at all, she knew that Rachel didn't say no to macaroni and cheese.

"Honey?" Charlotte was back at Rachel's door again. "Would you like a snack?"

Rachel appeared in the crack of her bedroom door. Her cheeks were blotchy from tears. "What kind of snack?"

"It's a surprise," Charlotte said. She sounded overly chipper.

Rachel groaned. "I'm not feeling well."

"Should I bring it up to you?"

Rachel lifted one shoulder toward her ear. Charlotte hustled back toward the staircase, anxious to use the macaroni and cheese as a balm against all the evils of the world. Maybe, once Rachel had a few spoonfuls in her, she would tell Charlotte everything that had gone wrong. Maybe they could solve it all together.

But when Charlotte returned to Rachel's with a heaping bowl of cheesy pasta, Rachel took one look at the bowl, scrunched her nose, and said, "I'm not that hungry."

Charlotte felt she'd been slapped in the face. "It's your favorite," she reminded her daughter, as though Rachel had forgotten.

"I'll have some later. Maybe."

Rachel then snuck the door closed, leaving Charlotte in the strange shadows of the hallway. She took a large bite of the steaming macaroni and chewed somberly. The top of her mouth was burnt in an instant. It was the kind of thing she would feel for days.

Back downstairs, Charlotte sat cross-legged at the kitchen table and tried to distract herself. Several emails came in from current clients, all of whom seemed to have the most annoying wedding-related questions on the planet. The *Lord of the Rings* girl wrote again to ask if they could have an announcer say, "One Ring to Rule Them All," as she and her husband slipped their rings over one another's fingers. Charlotte wanted to gag.

Around six, the front door opened. Everett hollered, "Honey, I'm home!" as a joke, pretending to be like a guy in a sitcom. Charlotte hustled to the foyer to watch as he slipped out of his rain gear, removed his shoes, and rushed toward her for a kiss. Their love ballooned around them. For a beautiful moment, she nearly forgot the panic she now had for Rachel.

"I have a surprise!" Everett said. He snuck his hand into his backpack and whipped out a magazine. "*National Geographic*" was emblazoned across the top.

"Is it out already?" Charlotte cried. She gripped the magazine and flipped through it, hungry for his story.

"It's the story directly in the center," Everett added, guiding her back toward the kitchen. Charlotte dropped into the kitchen chair just as she discovered his story. The cover image stretched across both pages, featuring a foggy Orcas Island and a gorgeous Main Street, where signs hung to illustrate the coziness of the village— the local bar, the local restaurant, and the local market. Charlotte's eyes filled with tears at the memory of their special days away. It had been a fantasy.

"Everett..." Charlotte breathed, reading the first few lines. His language came alive in her mind, building images and storylines that seemed transformative. Midway through the first paragraph, she lifted her gaze toward Everett's and said, "This is extraordinary."

Everett ripped his fingers through his hair. "It's the first time they've actually let me write. I always knew I could do more than photographs. It's such a thrill, Charlotte." He struck his arms into the air, looking like a triumphant football player.

Charlotte cackled and leaped into his arms. Pride overwhelmed her. As she embraced him and kissed his face, he continued to speak. His words were so jocular and hopeful. *How could she not believe in them?*

"And they asked me to head back next week to feature another part of the island!"

Charlotte immediately dropped back, gaping at him. "Next week?" She sounded like an injured animal.

"It won't be for long," Everett added hurriedly.

"You mean you've already agreed to it?" Charlotte wrapped a hand around her throat.

"I couldn't say no to something like that," Everett told

her. "It's for the online portion of the magazine, but it's still a huge deal. I want to be on their frequent rotation. You know?"

"And I take it they're not interested in Martha's Vineyard?"

"They featured it a few years back," he explained.

A wave of exhaustion barrelled over Charlotte. She collapsed back in the chair, propping her chin up on her fists. Everett sat across from her and placed his hand over hers. They held the silence for a long time. Charlotte felt like a child, protesting that she hadn't gotten her way.

"I'm sorry," she finally told him, shaking her head. "I really am so proud of you."

Everett stuttered. "What's going on?"

Charlotte rubbed her temples. "I overheard Rachel talking about some drama at school. It threw me into a panic..."

"The macaroni and cheese?" Everett pointed knowingly.

"She wouldn't even touch it," Charlotte told him.

Everett groaned and wrapped his hand tighter around hers. His presence calmed her immediately.

"I don't know what to do about it," Charlotte whispered.

"All you can do is offer your support, just as you already have," Everett reminded her. "She'll come out of her room when she's ready."

"We're just so close," Charlotte rasped. "It hurts me when she feels she can't come to me about whatever's going on."

"She's her own person," Everett reminded her. "Your relationship is a beautiful thing. But it's not her entire life."

"Why not?" Charlotte demanded, a sneaky smile lifting toward her ears.

Everett laughed good-naturedly. He dropped his lips over her hand and kissed it once, twice, and again. Charlotte's heart filled with love for him. How could she ever repay him for making her feel alive again?

"I really am so happy for you," Charlotte told him, swiping the tears from her eyes. "You're so talented."

But Everett just shoved all thought of that away. "I'm starving," he informed her. "And I've heard you make the best macaroni and cheese on Martha's Vineyard."

"Just on Martha's Vineyard?" Charlotte shot back. "Try the entire east coast."

Chapter Ten

S aturday, August 27th, was the Annual Oak Bluffs Birdwatching Convention. Wes had attended the convention every year since his girls had gone away, using it as a distraction from the big hole in his heart. Just last year, Kellan had agreed to attend, and Wes had paraded around with him, grateful for a young man to "show off" to the other birdwatchers. The other birdwatchers, most of whom were in the over-fifty club, commended Wes on bringing "youthful energy" into the group. Kellan had blushed any time he'd heard that; he'd probably felt like he'd stuck out like a sore thumb. Still, Kellan had spotted some remarkable birds during that particular outing and had announced their names proudly to the other birdwatchers, who'd looked at him bug-eyed, impressed. "He's a natural," another birdwatcher had muttered to Wes.

This year, however, Kellan was already off at the University of Massachusetts. He texted Wes about once a week, sending him a photograph of a bird he'd spotted on campus or discussing the intensity of his course load. Wes took each text message to heart and often grew anxious about how to respond. He didn't want to annoy Kellan too much, but he also didn't want the text messages to dry up.

A few days before the birdwatching convention was set to begin, Wes drummed up the courage to ask Beatrice to accompany him. They were out near Aquinnah Cliffside Overlook Hotel, which his niece, Kelli, had helped to restructure and design over the previous year. Their hiking shoes gripped the jagged rocks of the cliffside as they peered out across the frothing waves. Toward the Aquinnah Cliffside Overlook Hotel, several white trucks were parked— plumbers, painters, and what looked to be a piano mover. Wes burned with excitement to see the newly structured place, which had been destroyed in a hurricane back in the forties. His parents had met and fallen in love there, just as the hurricane had decided to have its way with them.

That had been so long ago, a time they couldn't return to no matter how much they wanted to. Wes and Kerry's parents had died long ago. Their stories were all that remained.

"A birdwatching convention?" Beatrice's blue eyes seemed to turn brighter when excited. "What doesn't this island have?"

"We seem to live pretty well without a whole lot of things," Wes countered. "Every time I leave the island, I notice that the rest of the world seems to 'need' a whole lot of junk that we don't."

"But a birdwatching convention is necessary," Beatrice teased.

"Maybe not necessary," Wes offered. "But it's a whole

lot of magic to get in a room with other people who love nature as much as you. I can tell you that."

"Then count me in," Beatrice told him. "I can't imagine a better way to spend a Saturday."

* * *

They agreed to meet outside the convention hall at seven-thirty in the morning. The convention hall was about a half-mile from downtown Oak Bluffs, a one-story building that often hosted weddings and family reunions. Amanda had agreed to drive Wes over that morning and now eased the car through the drop-off area, giving Wes a sleepy smile.

Amanda told him to call her if he needed a pick-up later on. "I'll just be with Sam," she explained. "Just up the road."

"Thanks, honey," Wes told her. "I can't think of a sweeter limousine service."

Amanda chuckled, watching him like a hawk as he stepped out of the car and into the shivery breeze of this late-August morning. He zipped his windbreaker to his chin and waved a sturdy hand as Amanda drove back to the main road. Around him, other birdwatchers ambled toward the visitor's center. They wore dark-colored backpacks with multiple compartments and had funny tans on their noses and eyes from binoculars and sunglasses.

Very soon, Beatrice emerged from the throng of other birdwatchers. She wore her gray hair loosely across her shoulders and adjusted her backpack across her shoulders. Her strides were confident, spritely. And when her eyes first found Wes's, they widened in recognition and joy.

"Aren't you a sight for sore eyes?" she said, giving him a side-hug.

Wes laughed. "None of us birdwatchers are much to look at. Except for you, of course."

Beatrice waved a hand, blushing. "Don't flatter me. Especially not before I've had a cup of coffee. Let's go."

Inside the visitor's center, other birdwatchers sat at round tables, sipped coffee from ceramic mugs, and nibbled on donuts that had been purchased from the Frosted Delights bakery in Edgartown. Beatrice instructed Wes to grab their seats. She disappeared for a moment, then returned with two mugs of coffee and two donuts, perfectly balanced on one of her outstretched palms.

"Multi-tasking," Beatrice explained as she set everything out across their table.

"Impressive." A voice rang out from the opposite end of the table. Wes lifted his head to find a broad-shouldered man in his late sixties seated across from them. Unlike the others around the visitor's center, this birdwatcher didn't have "nerdy characteristics." He didn't even have any ridiculous tan lines. He wore a pair of jeans and a navy button-down, and his hair was salt-and-pepper — more pepper than salt if Wes was honest.

The man was handsome in a way Wes hadn't been in some time.

It wasn't that Wes was fixated on his looks. Quite the opposite. He'd hardly thought about his looks in decades.

"Thanks," Beatrice returned, her voice like a song. "I waitressed in college."

"Where abouts?" the handsome man asked.

"I went to school in Boston," Beatrice explained. "About a million years ago." She sat next to Wes and sipped her coffee, but her eyes remained on their brand-new "friend."

"Boston. That's such a great town," the man replied. "I'm from the Midwest but came out east a few years ago."

"How do you find it?"

"It's God's country," the man told her.

"It really is." Beatrice's eyes glittered. "I just had the chance to move out to Martha's Vineyard this summer."

"This is your home?" The man looked flabbergasted. Wes thought it was all just an act, something to draw Beatrice closer to him. Wes had never been a "Casanova" type, but he'd seen them around. He had a hunch that Stan Ellis had been one back in the day. Wes assumed that accidentally killing the woman you were having an affair with would probably end your Casanova ways.

Beatrice tilted her head knowingly toward Wes. "He was born and raised here, so he's got us beat."

Wes grimaced. He felt terribly uncomfortable. Compared to this dashing Midwesterner with cool clothes and a full head of nearly black hair, Wes was nothing. The man clearly thought that, too. He hardly glanced his way when Beatrice brought him up. He stood and sauntered around the table, standing his full six-foot-four height. It was a rare thing for a man in his late sixties to be so tall.

"The name's Kurt," he told her, sticking out his hand.

Beatrice took it, smiling. "I'm Beatrice, and this is Wes."

Kurt hardly glanced Wes's way. "You two enjoy your morning. I'll see you later at dinner?"

"I've never missed a meal," Beatrice quipped.

Kurt's face broke into a joyous grin. Wes's stomach

tightened. Obviously, other men in the world weren't immune to Beatrice's ways. Jealousy was a strange thing to feel, especially at Wes's age. He wasn't sure how to hold it within him. It threatened to explode.

But Beatrice always had a way of rebounding. Just as soon as Kurt headed toward another group of bird-watchers to converse, Beatrice took a big bite of donut and began to chat about their plan for the day. First, they would drive out to the southern coast for a two-hour watch. Around lunch, they would attend a birding seminar back in town. After that, they would go for another birdwatching session, this time with a professional birder. As Beatrice talked and ate, bits of powdered sugar wound up on her lower lip. To Wes, she looked effortlessly adorable. All memory of Kurt drifted to the back of his mind. What did Kurt know about Beatrice? Wes's diary, which he'd packed in his backpack, was filled with information about Beatrice. Probably, if anyone ever found it, they would arrest Wes for stalking.

Wes and Beatrice waited around for the opening speeches from the birdwatching convention organizers, who discussed the intricate beauty of Martha's Vineyard and its precise ecosystem, which drew in the Ruddy turnstone species of birds. Wes found himself puffing out his chest with pride. It was true what Beatrice had said, that he'd been born and raised on the Vineyard. Others, like Kurt, traveled miles and miles to experience its beauty. Wes, on the other hand, had only to exit his back door.

Wes remained in good spirits throughout the morning. In the passenger seat of Beatrice's car (which she'd newly purchased that summer after her accident), Wes flicked through the radio stations and finally landed on a station from the seventies.

"Take it easy," Beatrice sang along with the Eagles' classic. "Take it easy..."

Wes joined her in singing, dropping his head back. A cool breeze slipped through the crack in the car window. For a long moment, Wes felt nothing but bliss. He wasn't sure he even deserved it.

"I just loved the music in the seventies," Beatrice said as the song petered out. "Gosh, I sound old just saying that."

"Sixties and seventies," Wes affirmed. "Everything turned to crap after that."

"You're right about that!" Beatrice cried.

The day continued on. As they wandered through the marshes and beaches of the south, Beatrice and Wes took photographs of birds to show off later at the convention and whispered to one another as the soft breeze wafted their gray hair back behind them. Sometimes, Beatrice's lips were so close to his cheeks as she whispered that Wes froze with fear. Suppose her lips accidentally brushed his skin.

Once, they locked eyes, listening to the rush of the water as it cascaded across the sand. Overhead, a bird twittered and cawed. Neither lifted their heads to look at it. But as they walked, Wes's hiking boot caught on a large branch. He turned his head to catch his balance, and when he returned his gaze to Beatrice, she was busy looking at the sky.

He'd missed his moment, whatever it was.

* * *

The visitor's center re-opened for the Birdwatching Convention Annual Dinner at seven o'clock. Beatrice parked the car in the first row, turned off the engine, and gave Wes a sidelong glance. Her cheeks were flushed.

"What a beautiful day," she said softly. "An entire day dedicated to birdwatching. Can you believe our luck?"

Wes felt like he was in high school. He imagined closing the distance between them, there in the front seat of her car. Hadn't he done that with Anna, all the way back in the seventies? Perhaps he'd been braver back then.

The visitor's center was bustling with birdwatchers, many of whom had even deeper tan lines than they had earlier that morning. A tray passed them with juice, wine, and beer, and both Wes and Beatrice took a glass of wine, clinking their glasses together. Wes explained that he didn't often drink much but that that night demanded celebration. Beatrice winked in agreement.

They grabbed seats in the middle, alongside a married couple from Louisiana who came up to Martha's Vineyard every year for the birdwatching convention. The couple was cheerful and chatty, showing off photographs they'd taken that afternoon and talking about one of their daughters— a girl in her twenties who went to college somewhere in Rhode Island. Wes hardly listened. After all, his mind could only take in so much information at once.

Beatrice seemed to hang on to their every word. She asked all the right questions, sipped her wine, and occasionally slipped in details about her own life. Her career as a naturopathy doctor thrilled them. The wife asked about the Katama Lodge and Wellness Spa and whether or not there were available slots the following week. With ease, Beatrice removed her business card and instructed the woman to give the Lodge a call to make an appointment.

"I'm so glad I met you!" the woman said, pocketing the business card.

Suddenly, a voice boomed over their heads. Wes nearly leaped from his skin.

"Aren't you Miss Congeniality?" the voice asked.

There he was: Kurt, from that morning. Naively, Wes had allowed himself to forget about him. He stood with a beer, so confident and sure of himself, and beamed down at Beatrice. He looked at her like he claimed her. The married couple from Louisiana lifted their eyes toward him and beamed, as well. Wes was basically a bump on a log.

"Hi there, Kurt!" Beatrice greeted him. "How was your day?"

Kurt stepped around and sat directly next to Wes, practically leaning over Wes's place to speak to Beatrice. "I saw a heron this morning," he said conspiratorially.

"Oh goodness," Beatrice breathed. "Aren't they captivating?"

Wes leaned far back in his chair and crossed his arms. The air in front of him stank of beer from Kurt's breath.

Wes drank his wine a little quicker than he'd planned to. His nerves made him jittery, and he found himself reaching for the glass, drinking it down, and setting it back down with a clunk. Despite all his best efforts, Kurt hardly noticed him at all. This enraged Wes all the more.

The servers for the birdwatching dinner arrived with the first course, a salad with goat cheese. Wes stabbed his fork through the leaves of his salad and watched as Beatrice lifted a forkful easily, her eyes dancing with laughter. Kurt was in the midst of yet another story, something about the birds in the Midwest.

"I know, it's a nightmare to get to," Kurt began, "but the rolling hills of Kentucky are really something to see. The wildlife is gorgeous. It's truly the heartland of America."

"How about that!" Beatrice said.

Even the married couple from Louisiana seemed captivated by him. Wes allowed his fork to drop back into his bowl of salad. He took another sip of wine as Beatrice launched into a story about an osprey she and Wes had seen that day. She said "we" but seemed not to glance at him at all. Wes felt like a ghost, watching his life from a distance.

The server arrived to take the salad bowls from the table to make space for the next course. He blinked down at Wes's salad, which he'd hardly touched. "Do you mind if I—" the server began.

But before he could finish, Wes leaped up from his chair. The chair clattered on the ground behind him. He lifted a handkerchief to his forehead as Beatrice blinked at him, confused.

"Wes? Are you all right?"

Wes's tongue tasted like sandpaper. *Had he actually thought that Beatrice felt something for him? Was he that naive?*

"I'll be right back," Wes told her, forcing a smile.

"Okay." She sounded doubtful. Probably, he looked like a fool. Just as he spun around to make his way to the back hallway and the subsequent bathrooms, Kurt distracted her with another tale about the goat cheese they made in Indiana and how it was "to die for."

When Wes reached the hallway, he collapsed against

the wall, his chest heaving. For not the first time when he couldn't breathe, he considered Anna's last moments. Water filling her lungs. She'd been unfaithful to Wes; she'd wronged their family. But God, he'd loved her. She hadn't deserved that.

Perhaps he would stew in his sorrows forever. Perhaps the hope he'd built for himself meant nothing at all.

Wes lifted his phone from his back pocket. With the flip of his thumb, he drew up Susan's phone number. Susan, his eldest— the one he could rely on. The one who'd first come home when his world had collapsed.

Too embarrassed to say the words he wanted to say aloud, Wes texted Susan.

> WES: Would you mind picking me up?

He could envision her that Saturday night, perhaps in front of the television with Scott or enjoying wine with her sisters on the back porch. Probably, since Wes was always such a burden to his daughters, they'd taken the opportunity of him having plans to do whatever they pleased. The text message brought that burden back onto her shoulders. Wes stewed in shame.

But Susan wrote back almost immediately.

> SUSAN: Where are you?

> WES: The visitor's center.

> SUSAN: I'll be there in ten. Sit tight.

Too embarrassed to remain in the hallway and fearful that Beatrice would come looking for him, Wes stepped into the chilly evening and stood along the sidewalk, watching the cars drift past. It was hard to believe that another summer on Martha's Vineyard would come to a close. He felt himself marching toward the doom of his life.

When Susan arrived, her brow was furrowed into a permanent line of worry. Wes buckled his seatbelt and stared straight ahead.

"Dad," Susan began, as though any line of words could help his mood.

"Please. Just take me home," Wes told her quietly.

Susan pressed the gas and did a U-turn at the next light. She drove wordlessly back toward the home she shared with Scott. Once in the driveway, she stopped the engine and heaved a sigh in the darkness.

"I really need to get some sleep," Wes muttered, surging his weight into the side of the door.

"Dad."

Something about the tone in Susan's voice gave Wes pause. Slowly, he turned around to blink through the darkness. He swallowed the lump in his throat.

"I thought we weren't doing secrets anymore," Susan whispered, her voice breaking.

But Wes didn't have the heart or the strength to tell her. His feet crunched through the gravel along her driveway as he headed toward the line of trees that separated their homes. A hand lifted, he said, "I love you, Susan. I really do."

Implied beneath his words was that he loved her, but even he couldn't face what had happened that night. The wind had been taken out of his sails. Perhaps his life was done.

Chapter Eleven

It was the last Tuesday of August. Outside Charlotte's office window, an orange leaf wafted on a nearby oak, taunting the other still-green leaves. The Vineyard Sound just beyond frothed ominously. Charlotte placed her fingers tentatively on the keyboard of her computer, her lips parted as she tore through the alleys of her mind for inspiration. Here it was— the two hours she'd set aside to think about the theme of her own wedding. And she was more than clueless.

Luckily, Everett picked this opportunity to distract her with a phone call from the west coast. Charlotte answered it hungrily.

"Hi, there!"

Everett's laughter rolled over her. "You sound happy. What are you up to?"

Charlotte blinked at her most recent online search: **"What should forty-something brides wear at their weddings, so they don't look absolutely ridiculous?"** Rachel had told her that the internet wasn't meant for literally asking such precise questions, but Charlotte had chosen to ignore that bit of advice.

"Nothing, really," Charlotte lied.

"You're never up to nothing," Everett countered.

"Ah, well. To be honest with you, I'm trying to create a wedding for a client based on her love for both *Game of Thrones* and *Lord of the Rings*. Not exactly my specialty."

Everett cackled. "But you're the best in the business. I know you'll find a way."

Charlotte dropped her head so that her brunette curls spilled over the back of the chair. Everett's voice was the nourishing force she'd so needed.

"Gosh, it's good to hear your voice."

"It's good to hear yours, too."

Charlotte's smile wrinkled her eyes. "Why did you leave me all alone out here on this lonely island?" she teased.

"I'll be back soon!" Everett said, his voice cracking. "Although, unfortunately, not as soon as I'd initially thought."

It felt like a stone dropped into the bottom of Charlotte's stomach. Her smile fell. "What do you mean?"

"The editor loved the interview and photographs from last weekend," Everett explained. "She wants a whole feature on the restaurant industry here on Orcas Island. I have an in with the chef we met, and he promised to take me around to all of his top favorite restaurants— including hole-in-the-wall places that haven't been written about. I can't help but feel like this is my chance, Char. My chance to finally prove myself as a real travel journalist and not just another photographer."

Charlotte's throat felt tight. She sipped her water as the silence brewed between them.

"Char? You still there?"

"I'm here." She shook her head violently, willing herself to snap out of it. "It sounds like a dream."

"It is my dream," Everett corrected. "It is. And I have to go for it." His voice felt heavy with purpose.

Charlotte knew him well enough to know he wouldn't ask for permission; he shouldn't have had to. She was a loving partner, an artist in her own right. Now that they were engaged, his successes were her successes.

"I'm proud of you," Charlotte heard herself say. "I can't wait to celebrate when you get back."

"Me too." Again, his voice was warm and inviting. "Tell me. How's it going with Rachel?"

Charlotte wrinkled her nose. "Her appetite comes and goes. She spends a lot of time in her room, brooding. I asked her for some help planning a wedding for next year, but she said something about doing her homework instead." Charlotte groaned and added, "We've always been so close, Ev. So close! I don't want our entire relationship to fall apart like this. It tears me up inside. And it makes me wonder if I missed something. Was I not paying attention?"

"She's seventeen," Everett reminded her. "Awash with hormones and terrified about the next stage of her life. You have to cut her some slack. Okay?"

Charlotte bit her lower lip. "I know that you're right. I just, ugh, want to snap my fingers and make her my bright and happy baby again."

* * *

A little while later, Charlotte found herself seated on the bench just outside Oak Bluffs High School. The bell had rung at three o'clock sharp, and almost immediately afterward, students had streamed out of it like water through a faucet. It was now three-twelve, and still no sign of Rachel, Gail, or Abby whatsoever. Charlotte told herself to keep her wits about her. Maybe Rachel was meeting with a teacher about an assignment she struggled with. Maybe she was involved in an after-school program that Charlotte had forgotten about (unlikely but still possible).

Charlotte's idea was that she would glide easily up to her daughter, chat with Rachel, Gail, and Abby, just like always, and eventually invite the girls out for milkshakes. This was something they'd done perhaps once a week in Rachel's younger years. *Why had that tradition stopped?*

Ultimately, this easy afternoon of milkshakes and conversations would lead Rachel to tell Charlotte what was on her mind. Together, Charlotte and Rachel would concoct a scheme to make whatever was wrong all right again.

This was Charlotte's fantasy. But as she watched the stream of teenagers ambling across the front grass of the high school, her stomach twisted with fear. There was something about these teenagers, something angry and alive. It had been a long time since her teenage years, but bits and pieces flung to Charlotte's mind— images of the scary yet beautiful cheerleading team, the jocks and the academics and the teachers who so often made you feel very small. Rachel was up against all of that and probably even more, especially with the rise of social media. Gosh, kids could be so cruel.

Charlotte no longer blamed Christine for this, but she remembered when Christine had teased her for never having been kissed. The shame of it had stirred in her gut for months. Jason had ultimately been her first (and, for a long time, last) kiss. The teasing had stopped, but the memory of the shame had remained.

Suddenly, there she was. Rachel stepped out of the high school with her spine bent forward to accommodate her massive backpack. Gail and Abby chattered to one another directly beside her as Rachel continued to stare at the grass. If she wasn't careful, she would probably trip and fall to her knees.

Charlotte stood with her hands clasped in front of her. She was no longer brave enough to penetrate the crowd of students and walk alongside her daughter. She had to wait for Rachel to step out onto the sidewalk.

As Charlotte waited, a group of teenage girls with sleek hair and short skirts cut past Rachel. One of them dipped their hips into Rachel, making her stumble. Charlotte's heart leaped into her throat. She felt frozen with fear. Another teenage girl leaped in front of Rachel and seemed to get into her face, speaking so that her nose was only an inch or so from Rachel's. Gail said something, trying to get between Rachel and the girl, but soon after, two other girls in the "squad" leaped between Rachel and Gail, creating a circle around her. Charlotte took several steps forward, terrified. This was a unique kind of rage, one without an answer. But just as Charlotte made up her mind to rush toward the girls and tear them apart, the teenage posse drifted away and then began to run. Their smiles were gorgeous, good enough for *Teen Vogue*. Rachel remained slumped forward, cupping her elbows. Gail and Abby huddled around her, comforting her. Rachel just shook her head in shame.

Charlotte leaped behind a tree and hustled around the side of a line of vehicles. She didn't want Rachel to know what she'd seen. After a long, dramatic pause, she rose up on her tiptoes and watched as Rachel, Gail, and Abby marched past her line of cars. She then rushed up to the front of the first vehicle and stepped out onto the sidewalk in front of them. She brought her arms out like a ballerina, making a mockery of herself.

"Mom?" Rachel sounded flabbergasted. "What are you doing here?"

"Hi, honey! Hi, Gail and Abby!" Charlotte sounded on the verge of a breakdown.

"Hi, Aunt Charlotte," the twins echoed, both confused.

Rachel adjusted her backpack over her slender shoulders. It took all of Charlotte's strength not to throw herself forward and wrap Rachel in a hug.

"Would you three like a milkshake? My treat," Charlotte recited carefully.

"You quit work early just to buy us milkshakes?" Rachel asked doubtfully.

"Don't tease me," Charlotte quipped. "You know how much I love milkshakes."

Rachel shrugged and glanced at her cousins. She was like a wounded animal. "What do you think?"

"We have to get home," Gail told them. "We promised Mom we'd help her with some flower arrangements."

Abby nodded vigorously. It wasn't clear if this was a lie, but Charlotte let them have it. "Get home safe, girls!" she called as they walked away.

This left Charlotte and Rachel alone at last. The only problem was that Rachel would hardly look at her mother. Even when they were seated across from one another at the local diner, Rachel hardly lifted her eyes. She ordered a strawberry milkshake, her favorite since she'd been a girl, but hardly dipped her spoon through the whipped cream. Charlotte continued to burn with a sharp rage, aching to know the identities of the bullying girls outside the school.

"So. How's your senior year going?" Charlotte finally asked.

Rachel shrugged. "It's going."

Charlotte arched her brow. "I was thinking. We need to shop for your Homecoming dress pretty soon!"

Rachel groaned. "I just started school. We have time."

Charlotte could hardly touch her chocolate shake. Her tongue felt overly sweet. The clock on the wall clicked toward four-fifteen, and an entire evening of silence prepared to stretch out in front of them. She should have searched for, "What to do when your daughter is being bullied in high school?"

When Rachel finished one-half of her milkshake, she removed her cell phone from her backpack and began to text someone furiously. Charlotte drummed up the courage to ask Rachel if she had any interest in helping with the upcoming wedding. Rachel shrugged and said, "Why not? I don't have anything else going on." Charlotte wasn't sure if that was code for something.

Later on, when they returned home from the diner, Rachel pounded her way up to her bedroom and closed the door. Charlotte was reminded of Christine, who'd been similarly moody and often alone in the dark shadows of her room. Christine hadn't "snapped out of it" until her forties. Charlotte prayed for a different fate for Rachel. She felt utterly helpless.

Chapter Twelve

That Friday, Charlotte had another anxiety-inducing conversation with her *Game of Thrones*-obsessed bride. "I really think I want everyone who comes to the wedding to be barefoot," she explained, her hands clasped near her chin. "It would complete the picture I have for the night."

Charlotte initially tried to explain to the bride that an all-barefoot wedding wasn't exactly up to the health code. But just as she formulated her argument, the bride burst into another rant about the rings she and her fiancé had picked out and how the artist hadn't exactly aligned with their vision. Charlotte held her tongue, thinking good and hard about abandoning this project once and for all.

By the time she jumped off the line, it was past three in the afternoon. Rachel texted to say that she planned to spend the afternoon with Gail and Abby before they headed to Grandpa Trevor and Grandma Kerry's. That night, the Montgomery clan planned to celebrate all things Isabella Montgomery, a girl on the precipice of the rest of her life. Tuesday, Laura planned to take the day off to take Isabella to her sublease apartment in Brooklyn. After that, her entire world would change forever.

As Charlotte had hardly left the island for more than a few nights at a time, she shivered with anxiety for Isabella's sake. Although the twenty-two-year-old girl seemed bright-eyed and optimistic, Charlotte could imagine the fear such a change had brought on. Had Charlotte been in Isabella's shoes, she wouldn't have slept a wink for many nights.

It was a warm day in early September, mid-seventies, with an eggshell blue sky above. September on Martha's Vineyard still beckoned heaps of tourists, all of whom bombarded the beaches and boardwalks and waterways— anxious to claim any last dregs of summertime. Strangely, Charlotte was ready for autumn, for cozy fires in the fire-place, warm wool socks, and thick sweaters. She longed for empty beaches and whipping winds and her mother's homemade clam chowder, which seemed to warm you deep down into your soul.

Charlotte donned a navy-blue sundress and packed a sweater in her backpack. With her hands in her dress pocket, she scampered out the front door of her home and walked down the sidewalk, loosening her aching joints. The walk to the Montgomery House, the gorgeous coastal Victorian where she'd grown up, was no more than twenty minutes, and she planned to daydream the entire way. The goal was to force all thoughts of bridezillas and volatile mothers-of-the-brides from her mind and dream up a gorgeous vision for her own wedding. What sort of wedding screamed "Everett and Charlotte"?

Along the route to her parents' place, Charlotte found herself only a block or so away from Steve's mechanic shop. Curious, she popped over and peeked her head between the dark shadows of two slightly busted vehicles, one of which had been lifted into the sky. A mechanic worked beneath it, his tools clanking against the innards of the car.

"Hi, stranger," Charlotte teased Steve's tennis shoes, which were covered with grime.

Steve lifted his shoes and cackled. His laughter echoed around the inside of the vehicle. "Is that my kid sister?"

"You'd better get yourself cleaned up," Charlotte said. "I heard we have a big family party tonight."

Steve eased himself out from beneath the car. His smile was electric, his white teeth shining between his cheeks, which had been stained with oil and whatever else his career had gifted him. His strong arms extended on either side as he said, "You want a hug before that clean-up?"

Charlotte tossed her head back. "Not unless you're a glutton for punishment."

Steve grabbed a half-clean towel from a hanging rack in the corner and sponged it at his face. "What's been going on, Little Sis?"

Charlotte scrubbed her sandal across the pavement. "I was heading to Mom and Dad's place early. Thought Mom might want some help with the cooking."

"Aren't you sweet?" Steve teased her. "You know that Mom doesn't share that kitchen well."

"She'd better learn," Charlotte offered.

"When was the last time Kerry Montgomery learned a thing?" Steve asked. "She's as stubborn as an ox."

"She passed that along to her children," Charlotte said. "Especially her eldest."

"Ha." Steve dabbed his towel across his neck, picking up sweat. "Laura's been a mess about Isabella's move."

"I can't imagine," Charlotte breathed. "Next year, if Rachel heads off the island, you'll hear me crying myself to sleep every night from four streets over."

"It's been about the same at my place," Steve said. His eyes grew shadowed. "I'm sure Laura would appreciate any kind words, you know. I feel like I can't say anything right."

"Husbands can never say anything right," Charlotte shot back, smiling. "It's the law of the land."

"Can't imagine what it'll be like when we finally get a woman in the White House," Steve teased as he tossed the towel back on the hook. "Not that I'm complaining. Laura runs our household; Mom runs hers. The women in the family are the strongest people I know. My guess is that it extends across the whole world."

"You got that right." Charlotte shared a toothy smile, her heart ballooning with love for her family.

A customer arrived shortly after to discuss the next steps Steve needed to take to fix his car. Charlotte took this opportunity to head to their mother and father's house. A hand raised, she hollered, "See you later!" as Steve prepared to leap beneath the dirty car again. It occurred to Charlotte, not for the first time, that Steve and Charlotte had opposite jobs— hers was all about fresh flowers and beautiful moments and white dresses, while his was grime and gook and violent-looking tools. The Montgomery Family was a funny hodgepodge of talented individuals. No two members were the same.

* * *

After some humming and hawing, Kerry allowed Charlotte into her kitchen and put her to work on last-minute dinner preparations. The radio sputtered the oldies' station, playing everything from Hall and Oates to John Mellencamp to Dolly Parton. Kerry sang "Working 9 to 5" under her breath as she gathered plates to set the table. Meanwhile, out back, Trevor worked on the garden with Jonathon, Isabella's older brother, who often helped his grandfather with tasks around the house.

"They're good kids," Kerry said under her breath, poised in the window.

"Who?" Charlotte asked.

Kerry's eyes glittered. "All of our grandchildren are remarkable humans. Jonathon swings by to help about twice a week. Rachel, Gail, and Abby were just here a few days ago to help me hang the bedsheets on the clothesline. Watching them pin the bedclothes, I thought about my mother and I, performing that same task. It feels like just two weeks ago. Goodness, she's been gone so long."

Charlotte's heart felt squeezed. She continued to slice and dice the red peppers for the vegetable platter, blinking several times to keep her tears at bay.

"What do you think about Isabella going off to Brooklyn?" Charlotte heard herself ask her mother a little while later.

Kerry tossed her hair flippantly. "I don't know what anyone could possibly find off the island. We have so much here, don't we?"

Charlotte had to admit, she agreed. But she could imagine Isabella's curiosity.

"Then again, Isabella was always such a wild card,"

Kerry continued, giving Charlotte a mischievous smile. "Her father and mother never knew what to do with her."

"People get married older and older," Charlotte reminded her mother.

"Yes. It's not how we used to do it back in the old days," Kerry continued, loosening her shoulders. "I can't help but wonder if it gets lonely, not settling down." She dried her hands on a kitchen towel and stepped closer to Charlotte. "But listen to me. I'm just an old woman, prattling on about things I don't know anything about. What about you, Charlotte? How are you doing, anyway? I've hardly seen you since the engagement party at Susan's."

Charlotte's lips broke into a smile. Her engagement ring became heavy on her finger, and she lifted it to flash it in the late afternoon light.

"Everett really knows how to pick out jewelry," Kerry said, impressed. "If your father was tasked with buying me a simple bracelet, he'd probably leave the jewelry store with a keychain that said 'Go Red Socks' on it and call it a day."

Charlotte howled with laughter, gripping the edge of the counter. Her mother was probably right. Before she could fully compose herself, the front door screamed open, and the voice of Laura cascaded through the air.

"Hello? Is anyone home?"

"In here, honey!" Kerry called her daughter-in-law. "You can have the front row seat for Charlotte losing her mind."

Charlotte heaved, trying to pull herself together. She forced herself forward to hug Laura, whose cheeks and eyes were blotchy with tears.

"You poor thing," Charlotte said, her laughter immediately dying. She rubbed Laura's back as Kerry fetched a bottle of chardonnay from the fridge.

Laura accepted a glass, scrunching her nose. "I gave myself a pep talk on the way here. I said, 'Laura, it's a family party. Don't break down.' But here I am."

"Pish-posh," Kerry said. "It's only Charlotte and I. You don't have to hide away from us."

Laura sipped her chardonnay with her eyes closed so that her thick eyelashes swept across her cheeks. "Isabelle has insisted on bringing just one suitcase and one backpack. To build a whole new life!"

"Can you imagine trying to put all your belongings in a suitcase and a backpack?" Kerry asked Charlotte.

Charlotte arched her brow. "Mom, I'm not overly materialistic..."

Kerry spoke conspiratorially to Laura. "She begged me to buy three prom dresses for her, just in case she changed her mind about which one to wear on the day of prom."

"Oh, I did not."

"She was just a fancy girl," Kerry said, her smile widening. "It's served her well." After a beat, she added, "And your Isabella knows best about her life, as well. If she thinks just a suitcase and a backpack will work for her life in the big city, she'll make it work. You have to trust her, now. She's out of the nest."

Laura's chin quivered. "I know you're right. But you might have to give me a few more pep talks over the next few weeks. Anything to get me through."

"We'll be your coaches through this," Kerry affirmed. "Just give us a call or stop by. We always have time for a chat or a glass of wine." She winked, grabbed her own glass, and swirled the liquid.

* * *

The rest of the guests arrived around six o'clock that night. They came in a steady stream: first Steve, all scrubbed clean and dressed in a polo shirt and a pair of jeans; next, Andy, Beth, her son, Will, and their brand-new baby, who slept peacefully against Beth's chest. Next came Kelli and her daughter, Lexi. Isabella, the guest of honor, arrived at six-fifteen, her own eyes blotchy with tears but her smile overcompensating for her obvious fear.

Charlotte jumped up to hug her niece, who shivered against her and then burst into a tirade about rent prices in Brooklyn and the fact that her new roommate (whom she'd found online) was vegan and insisted that there be "no meat products in the house." Laura scoffed at this, saying, "Hasn't she ever had clam chowder? Hasn't she ever lived?"

Isabella laughed and puffed out her cheeks.

"It'll be fine," Charlotte told her, rubbing her shoulder. "When you get a craving for a hamburger, just eat a hamburger. Outside, of course."

"Most hamburgers are twenty-five dollars," Jonathon reminded his sister with a laugh.

"Ha," Isabella shot back. She stuck her tongue out at him as he hustled past to care for his own child, who'd begun to cry.

"Mom!" Rachel called from the foyer, where she, Gail, and Abby removed their shoes. She looked brighter than she had the previous week, as though all memory of that horrific after-school milkshake had melted away. Charlotte leaped over to hug her daughter close. Around her, a chorus of conversation buzzed.

This was family. This was where she felt the most love.

They feasted on lemony salmon, Brussels sprouts, homemade biscuits, mashed potatoes, and plenty of wine. Trevor sat at the head of the table and held court for much of the evening, often finding ways to bring Isabella into the conversation. After all, she was supposed to be the central focus for the night.

After dinner, Charlotte, Kerry, and Claire hustled around, collecting dirty plates. There was a homemade strawberry rhubarb pie in the fridge— enough to go around. Kerry removed it just as Trevor began to clank his fork against the outer glass of his wine.

"I'd like to say a few words about our girl, Isabella," Trevor began, tilting his head lovingly.

On the other side of Isabella, Steve wrapped his arm around Laura. Tears welled in her eyes and streamed down her cheeks. He pressed a kiss on Laura's forehead, his eyes heavy with love and emotion. Charlotte had to look away; it seemed too private.

"The past twenty-two years, our Isabella has been a force of nature," Trevor began. "I remember when she used to run around on the beach, making me time her as she hustled from one tree to another about fifty feet down. Even two hours later, it seemed like she couldn't physically get tired."

"Only for her to collapse on the couch a little while later," Kerry chimed in. "All covered in cookie crumbs."

Isabella chuckled, her cheeks turning pink. Charlotte knew the embarrassment of being talked about like this. She'd felt it in spades at her own engagement party; it had brought up memories of her wedding all those years ago.

"What I mean to say is this. Isabella, you never ran

out of energy. You always wanted more of everything: more of life, more noise, more spirit, and more laughter. When your father first told us that you wanted to leave the island, I told him that it made a lot of sense to me. This island can't possibly contain you, Isabella. Go out into the world and show them what kind of girl— no, woman— you are. You're a Montgomery, after all. The world needs to know."

Tears stained the top of Isabella's dress. Laura burrowed her face into Isabella's shoulder as the rest of the table cried, "I'll drink to that!" Charlotte dropped off another stack of plates in the kitchen, grabbed her glass of wine, and lifted it toward Isabella. She locked eyes with her niece, her heart lifting. This was a pivotal moment.

It felt incredible to be a part of the magic of this young woman's life.

It made Charlotte believe in magic of her own.

Chapter Thirteen

Everett called Charlotte that Sunday evening with more "incredible" news.

"I have another interview scheduled for Monday afternoon," he said. "With this best-of-the-best chef based on Lopez Island. Apparently, he hasn't taken a single interview in over ten years."

Charlotte perched at the edge of the back porch, a glass of wine sweating on the picnic table. Now that Everett had been out west for the past couple of weeks, it was hard to imagine that they'd ever shared this very table. She'd grown accustomed to reading at the table alone.

"That's fantastic news," she told her fiancé, her heart pounding. "I mean, how did you even manage to wrangle that interview?"

Everett continued on, describing the elaborate coincidences that had had to occur for him to nab the interview. Charlotte echoed his excitement, even as she sunk deeper in sorrow. For not the first time that weekend, Charlotte found herself awash with fears about the future. *What if*

Everett decided never to come home? Was their love actually enough?

"I love you, baby," Everett told her before they got off the phone. "I wouldn't have been able to do any of this without you."

Charlotte wasn't so sure that was true. "I love you back. Hope to see you this week?" She hardly dared to ask.

"Of course! What would I do without my Vineyard gals?" Everett returned. "Tell Rachel that I'll be there soon. I can beat up whoever's been bullying her."

Charlotte groaned. "Don't mention that to her. Okay? I want to give her privacy, at least for now."

Charlotte felt she'd know, intuitively, when to "step in" when it got too difficult for Rachel. This was probably naive.

Rachel was on the couch, chewing at the end of a large pretzel and flicking through channels. Charlotte closed the door and wandered up behind her, catching sight of Rachel's glazed eyes.

"Are you okay?"

Rachel shrugged. It was like Charlotte's question had been the stupidest in the history of the world. "Yeah."

"Mind if I watch with you?"

Rachel dropped her head toward the couch cushion, allowing it to nestle in the soft fabric. Charlotte stepped around and sat just as Rachel decided on a home makeover show. A man with a sledgehammer smashed through old cabinets, sending splintering wood into the corners.

"I'd love to do that," Rachel said.

"Really?" Charlotte had never known her daughter to be violent.

Rachel nodded. "Wouldn't it be awesome to just destroy something like that? You could get all your emotions out."

Silence stretched between them as the man on the television continued to whack and destroy. Charlotte was reminded of toddlers who wanted to wreak havoc on everything around them. A few minutes later, she heard herself ask Rachel if she wanted a snack of some kind, but Rachel lifted her half-eaten pretzel, clearly annoyed. Charlotte couldn't do anything right. And on top of it all, Everett would probably never come home again.

"I'm heading to bed," Charlotte finally said, her voice cracking.

"It's eight," Rachel said.

"I'm just ready to end the day," Charlotte said. "Good night." She paused at the staircase, her palm flat across the wall. "And Rachel? I love you. You know that, right?"

Rachel's voice was on-edge. "I know."

She didn't say it back.

* * *

That Tuesday afternoon, Charlotte met with a bride whose wedding approached later that month. The bride had whittled herself down to a size four and, even now, sucked on a green smoothie, her cheeks pale from lack of sustenance. It always made Charlotte sad to see brides like this. She so often wanted to hug them and tell them that weddings were supposed to be about love— not about the kind of self-hatred required to make yourself very small.

After the meeting, Charlotte headed home and sat on the front porch, going over her notes. It was three-fifteen, and soon, Rachel would return home. Charlotte had a half-plan in mind for the afternoon and evening ahead. First, she'd suggest that they paint their toenails and fingernails and discuss current celebrity gossip. Next, they'd sit on the beach for a round of mocktails. Somewhere between their first sip and the last, Rachel would get up the nerve to tell Charlotte what was going on at school.

Hadn't they always been thicker than thieves? Hadn't their mother-daughter relationship been more like a friendship, especially lately?

Three-twenty came and went. Charlotte burrowed herself in her notes, ignoring the lateness of the hour. Distracted, she rewrote notes and underlined "important" lines while her heart pounded in her chest.

At three-forty, Charlotte's heart leaped into her throat. *Where was Rachel?*

Charlotte grabbed her cell, nearly dropping it as she tore it from the tabletop.

> CHARLOTTE: Hey honey! What's up? Did you head to Gail and Abby's?

After the message was sent, Charlotte gaped at her phone for a full minute, praying for Rachel's quick message in return. It didn't come.

"Hmm."

Charlotte decided next to break the cardinal sin of phone etiquette. She decided to call her daughter. But after only two rings, the phone cut to voicemail. *What the heck was going on?*

Charlotte leaped from the front porch picnic table and hustled inside. Her thoughts ran wild as she grabbed her purse, stabbed her feet into her sandals, and rushed out the front door. Halfway to Claire's flower shop, she realized where she was headed. It was a strange thing to feel that your body had made plans without letting your brain know.

The bells that hung from the top of the front door jangled joyously. Charlotte burst through the crack in the door, gasping for air. Inside Claire's flower shop, John Mayer sang his soft pop hits from the mid-two-thousands. Back then, Claire and Charlotte had played his CDs on repeat, swooning at the romance of his voice. Jason had teased them to no end.

"Charlotte?" Claire popped out from the back room carrying a handful of daisies. The flowers bobbed and jumped, and their leaves were overly long, in need of a chop before they found their rightful place in a bouquet or arrangement.

Charlotte rushed through the space between them, inhaling the gorgeous and thick floral air. Claire's smile dropped as Charlotte burrowed herself in Claire's arms.

"What's going on?" Claire asked.

"Oh, gosh. I'm sure it's nothing," Charlotte said, stepping back. She grabbed a tissue from the counter and dabbed her forehead, which was beady with sweat.

Claire placed the daisies on the counter and lifted her hair into a ponytail with a flourish. "The sooner you tell me about this 'nothing' situation, the sooner I can help you fix it."

Charlotte let out a single hiccup-laugh. "I probably just misremembered Rachel's plans."

"Yeah?" Claire's brow furrowed. "She didn't come home?"

"I mean, obviously, the girls are just all together somewhere," Charlotte heard herself continue, waving her hand. "Wherever one of them goes, the other follows. I know that."

Claire's face was lined with shadows. She walked around Charlotte and pulled open the door between the front of the shop and the back. "Girls?" she called. "Can you come out here for a minute?"

Charlotte watched with bated breath as first Gail, then Abby stepped into the soft light of the flower shop. Above them, John Mayer continued to croon. Charlotte had never detested the sound of his voice more.

"Hi, girls!" Charlotte didn't want to sound insane. "Have you seen my daughter this afternoon?"

Abby sucked on a bright green sucker. She popped it out to say, "Rach said she had to get home."

Gail nodded. "Yeah. Something about homework."

Charlotte stumbled back toward the door. Her eyes filled with tears. Claire leaped forward, cupping Charlotte's elbow.

"Char, it's okay. I'm sure there's another explanation."

Charlotte was reminded of those first few hours after she'd learned of Jason's death. Claire's eyes had been similar to how they were now— big and wide and fearful, watching Charlotte as though she were a porcelain doll falling to the ground.

"Let me call her," Gail shot out, pressing her phone to her ear. Apparently, the cardinal sin of calling didn't extend to your peers.

They waited, watching as Gail's face transformed from certainty to one of confusion. "That's so weird. She always answers us."

"She must be somewhere," Claire blared at her daughters. "Come on, Gail. Abby. Use the brains that

116

God gave you and think. We need a list of any possible place she could be."

Gail and Abby caught one another's eyes. Charlotte had the strangest sensation that they were communicating with bizarre "twin" language.

"There's something going on at school. Isn't there?" Charlotte muttered, just barely loud enough to hear.

"She would have told us if she was doing something insane," Abby shot out.

Charlotte grabbed a strand of her hair, tugging and twirling it. A few strands popped from her skull. Far, far away, on the west coast, the man who'd asked her to pledge her entire life to him expanded his career, took photographs, and ate four-course meals. She felt terribly alone, perhaps more so, even, than before she'd met Everett. At least back then, she'd had Rachel by her side.

After another minute of prodding, Gail and Abby came up with a list of potential spots. Rachel didn't have a car, so unless she had run off with someone from school (or, God forbid, a stranger), she probably hadn't walked far. Charlotte typed the list out on her phone:

Diner

Movie Theater

Sunrise Cove Inn

Sheridan Law Office (seen speaking with Amanda recently at a family party)

Coastal Beaches

Bars (free drinks from unsuspecting tourists?)

It was like finding herself in a nightmare. Charlotte rushed from the flower shop with hardly a "goodbye" and flung herself headlong toward the nearby diner. Behind her, Claire called, "We'll go out looking, too!"

Charlotte waved back, calling out words that were soon swallowed up by her own tears.

As she raced, Charlotte's phone began to ping and buzz with messages from other members of her family. Apparently, Claire had acted quickly, calling in the troops to search for her darling girl. When Rachel learned about this, she would be so embarrassed. *"I can't believe you made such a fuss, Mom,"* she would say accusingly.

Charlotte prayed Rachel would be angry. She prayed that she would pick a fight and stomp to her bedroom. She prayed she would have the opportunity to ground Rachel for perhaps the first time. All of that would mean that Rachel was actually okay.

> ANDY: Hey! I'm leaving the warehouse now. I'll drive around Edgartown to see if she's around. Stay strong, sis. We'll find her. I promise.

> KELLI: Teenagers do this. They get carried away with their emotions and ride them as long as they'll go. But we'll find her!

> KELLI: Leaving the Aquinnah Cliffside now and will search along the coastlines.

> STEVE: Hey! I'm sending some of the boys at the auto shop out to look for Charlotte. They just graduated and have a hunch about where a senior in high school might hide.

> STEVE: Meanwhile, I'm on the hunt, too. I'll keep you updated.

Charlotte was too frantic to respond to her siblings. She paused at the stoplight, clenched her eyes closed, and nearly collapsed with worry. Again, she grabbed her phone to try to call Rachel. But this time, the other end of the line didn't ring at all.

The diner was bustling with after-school traffic. A high school couple in the corner seemed unwilling or unable to rise up from their make-out session. Charlotte demanded of the first server she could get the attention of, "Have you seen Rachel Hamner?" It was a small town, after all; everyone knew everyone else. But the server just brushed Charlotte off, heading for the back window to pick up three banana milkshakes.

Charlotte waited outside the diner for four anxious minutes, watching the crowds of tourists stream past. Frequently, she glanced back into the diner to take stock of the diners. Perhaps Rachel had been in the bathroom? Perhaps she'd dyed her hair bright pink? But after four minutes, Charlotte couldn't justify her time at the diner any longer. She walked back into the sun and headed across the street and four blocks over to a coffee shop that Rachel had once said was "okay." *Was that enough of a lead? How much power could Charlotte give to any of her memories?*

After a half-hour of manic walking and the occasional running spurt, Charlotte collapsed against a red brick wall. She texted Claire to say: "No luck. You?" But when Claire texted back, "We're still looking. It won't be long now," Charlotte shoved her phone back in her pocket and very nearly gave up hope.

How many teenagers ran away from home? Charlotte had to assume there were loads of them. Hadn't Susan, Christine, and Lola all fled the Sheridan House at the first sight of locked land? Perhaps, with whatever was going on at the high school, Rachel had decided that whatever lurked out there was better than the evil of her everyday life.

How could Charlotte translate just how stupid that was?

Texts came in from her siblings, her mother, and her father.

> TREVOR: No sign of her at the Sunrise Cove or Susan's law office.

> KERRY: Wes and Audrey haven't seen her anywhere.

> STEVE: No sign of her in all of downtown Edgartown. I've been walking around for over an hour. I would have spotted her by now.

> KELLI: Lexi is searching, now, as well.

Charlotte shoved her phone deeper into her pocket, cursing to herself. She began to drag herself forward, her heart thudding. Without rhyme nor reason or any plan at all, she wandered the island streets, eyeing tourists with particular interest. A part of her thought that maybe if she just looked at people hard enough, they would automatically transform into her daughter. This wasn't rational. Maybe she was going insane.

At five-twenty-five, Charlotte paused briefly at a little snack stand near the boardwalk to buy a bottle of water. She drank the water in a single go and tossed it in the recycling bin. The water loosened her mind; more concrete thoughts came to her— about going to the police, notifying Rachel's teachers, and having some kind of vigil, something that allowed the public to come together.

Oh, God. No. She shoved these thoughts from her mind and bent her face toward her hands. Her heart thudding, she tried to put herself in the mind of her daughter. Rachel was in the midst of something horrible, a teenage drama that Charlotte couldn't comprehend. Where would a girl like that go?

Charlotte collapsed on a bench near the snack stand and hunted for her phone. In a flash, she had Claire on the other line.

"Hey." Claire was out of breath. "Any luck?"

Charlotte was crushed. "Where are you looking now?"

Claire groaned. "We're near the Katama Lodge. Now that she's been gone since school got out, she could have walked a great distance." Claire lowered her voice to add, "My twins are falling apart. They've never seen this out of Rachel. I've asked them a few times about the drama at the high school, but they just shove it aside, telling me it's just high school drama. Stuff I wouldn't understand."

Charlotte's eyes welled with tears. "Tell them that it's important, Claire. Tell them that it'll help us find her."

Claire was clearly exasperated. She brought her phone away from her face so that her voice became muffled as she called back in the car to her twins. "It's so important, girls. So important. We need to know everything that's gone on lately at the high school. We need to find your cousin. Please."

"It's just a boy problem!" Gail shrieked before falling into tears of her own. Beside her, it sounded like Abby burst into her own round of tears. Neither seemed ready to talk. Charlotte wanted to scream at them, to tell them how essential this really was.

But while Charlotte's anger mounted, Claire sounded only frightened. "Girls. Please. Please, stop crying. It's all right." A second later, the phone was back in front of her mouth, so that a loud, "I need to call you back, Charlotte. We'll keep looking. Don't give up hope. She has to be around here somewhere," came through the speaker.

When Claire hung up the phone, Charlotte sat, alone and despondent, as the tourists near the Oak Bluffs board-walk breezed past her. Their cheeks were sun-kissed; many carried popsicles and ice cream cones. Their laughter was a cacophony, filled with joy.

Charlotte wondered for the first time in quite a while if she would experience joy ever again. Her imagination had its way with her. The future seemed entirely bleak.

Charlotte forced herself back to her feet. Her arms crossed tightly over her chest, she wandered like a lost dog across the boardwalk, blinking back tears. Six in the evening came, then six-fifteen. All the while, her family members updated her with the nothingness of their own search parties. She didn't bother to write back.

Around seven-thirty, a gooey pink sunset brewed across the sky. Charlotte marveled at the beauty the world could give you, even as it allowed such destruction. She paused at the far end of the boardwalk, alongside the Oak Bluffs carousel. The music of the carousel seemed ominous and cartoony; Charlotte could remember a time when the song had been nothing but joyful and heavy with nostalgia.

Very near to where she stood, the ferries disembarked from the island and headed toward Woods Hole. Tourists passed their suitcases off to ferry dock workers, adjusted their ball caps and polos, and stepped onto the mighty ferries. You could see the sorrow in their eyes: vacation was over, and no matter how many times they looked at the photographs they'd taken or told the same stories over and over, they could never get that vacation back.

Charlotte had never experienced leaving Martha's Vineyard without plans to come back. What a sorrowful feeling, watching the mighty green rock disappear on the horizon. That "rock" held everything Charlotte had ever known. It was where she'd fallen in love, gotten married, and given birth. It was where Jason was buried, where she'd met Everett, and where she'd decided to trust in a second chance.

Toward the edge of the ferry docks stood the ferry offices. Tourists lined up to purchase tickets from a woman behind the counter. Each purchase seemed to take a tiny infinity, as though the ticket-seller enjoyed hearing every single story from every single tourist. Charlotte imagined that was part of the job— enjoying the many characters who breezed in and out.

And then, something caught Charlotte's eye.

A teenage girl sat at a picnic table directly next to the ferry ticket office. She had her chin propped up on her fists, and she peered out at the ferry that had recently departed. She seemed captivated with the departure, as though a part of her craved to get on the next ferry and duck out of sight.

Even before Charlotte fully realized it was Rachel, she felt her legs rip forward. She ran faster than she ever remembered running, so fast that her thighs and calves screamed. As she burst toward the picnic table, Rachel turned her beautiful head toward her to show the glistening tears in her eyes.

Charlotte didn't have time to be angry. She collapsed on the picnic table beside her daughter, wrapped her arms around her, and burrowed her head on her shoulder. Rachel hiccupped with sorrow and then began to cry fully. Her body shook within Charlotte's embrace.

All the while, ferries disembarked and returned to the island, back and forth from the mainland. The sounds were strange. A group of hundreds stepped onto a ferry, and their noise seemed impenetrable and all-encompassing. No more than five minutes after disembarking, the sounds of their laughter and chatter had completely ceased.

This left only Charlotte, only Rachel.

Finally, Charlotte lifted her head and opened her eyes. Rachel followed suit. They held one another's gaze for a long time until Charlotte dared herself to speak.

"I'm so glad you're okay."

Rachel's chin wiggled with sorrow. "I just wanted to go for a walk."

Charlotte shoved down her rage. It wasn't a useful tool. "Honey, it's after seven. You didn't tell anyone where you were going."

"I know." Rachel dropped her shoulders forward.

"Rachel, you've been so quiet. So quiet," Charlotte breathed. "We used to tell each other everything. What happened? Why can't you open up to me anymore?"

Rachel hiccupped. Her eyes were large and hollow. "I want to tell you everything."

"Why don't you?" Charlotte demanded. "I was a teenager once, you know."

"That's what everyone says," Rachel breathed.

Charlotte rolled her eyes. "I'm not everyone. I'm your

mother. As far as I can tell, we've been through a lot together. Why not this, too?"

Rachel eyed the picnic table. Paint chips had peeled from the top, proof, maybe, that summer was soon officially over. Things on the island tended to fall apart toward the end.

Charlotte became vaguely aware that her phone was buzzing. She jumped slightly, reaching for it. When she removed it from her pocket, STEVE appeared on the front of her cell.

"Everyone's out looking for you," Charlotte explained softly.

"Mom? Are you serious?" Rachel looked mortified. All the color drained from her cheeks.

Charlotte wanted to say something flippant like, *"What did you expect?"* But she kept that to herself. It wouldn't do any good.

Charlotte answered Steve's call. Her voice was bouncy, relieved. "Hey, Steve. Guess who I'm sitting next to at the ferry docks?"

Immediately after, silence followed. For a long time, Charlotte thought that Steve had just accidentally buttdialed her. "Steve? Are you there? Steve?"

Across from her, Rachel furrowed her brow. "What's wrong?" she whispered.

Finally, a wail came out of the darkness. "Charlotte..."

Charlotte had never heard her older brother sound like that. She leaped from the picnic table and shoved a finger on her opposite ear. "Steve, what's wrong? Are you okay?"

Sometimes, in the Montgomery family, it felt like running from one disaster to the next.

All Steve could do was wail. He hiccupped and wept, sputtering words that Charlotte couldn't understand.

"Steve? Where are you? Just tell me where you are so that I can come to help you," Charlotte demanded. She tried to sound authoritative, but in reality, she probably just sounded terrified.

Rachel's skin was the color of parchment. Charlotte's own eyes filled with tears that now ran down both cheeks. Finally, Steve came out with his location— he was parked at the Sunrise Cove Inn. He needed someone. Anyone. He couldn't be alone.

"We'll be there as soon as we can," Charlotte echoed as she leaped to her feet.

"Stay on the phone," Steve cried. "I can't be alone like this, Charlotte. I don't know how. I just don't."

Chapter Fourteen

Chapman Funerals and Cremations in Oak Bluffs was painted a harsh white. That Friday, it caught the sunlight, throwing sharp rays into Charlotte's eyes. Charlotte, whose arms were heavy with Claire's flowers, nearly stumbled on the walkway as she headed toward the propped-open front door. Behind her, Claire cried, "Charlotte! Be careful!"

It was a silly thing, hearing "be careful." Charlotte minded her footsteps and walked slowly up the little porch staircase before heading into the floral-smelling funeral home. Every corner echoed with her own memories of Jason's funeral, but she kept her eyes trained ahead as Claire instructed her to head into the main room and position the flowers to the right of the coffin.

The coffin remained closed for now. With the flowers out of Charlotte's arms, she stood and gazed at the shining wood of the coffin. Steve had selected the coffin in a hurry, wanting to get the week done and over with. Charlotte could hardly remember the decisions she'd had to make after Jason's death. She supposed, in many ways, those decisions didn't fully matter. They were things you "had" to do to start the grieving process. In reality, the grieving process was a varied and dark journey, one that went on long after the funeral doors were locked up for the night.

Claire appeared at Charlotte's side, her hands on her hips. "I still can't believe it," she breathed, eyeing the coffin.

"She was so young," Charlotte whispered. She took a dramatic step toward the first row of chairs and collapsed, pressing her chin onto her fist. Claire joined her and leaned back on the chair; shadows lined her face, making her look exhausted. Charlotte probably looked the same.

It was a difficult thing watching your eldest brother fall through the stages of grief. After Jason's death, Charlotte had hardly given her siblings a thought. She'd had to keep herself and her daughter alive. Probably, it had been horrific for her siblings to watch. This wasn't anything she'd considered, not till that week. In fact, if she was honest, she hadn't thought that anyone else in her life could possibly die— not after the tremendous pain of the past few years. How naive she'd been.

"Hey." A voice rang out from the far end of the funeral home. Charlotte and Claire turned back to find their little brother Andy, dressed in a newly pressed suit. He tapped the back of chairs as he walked toward them, limping slightly. His war injury was ever-present.

Charlotte stood and hugged Andy. Claire followed. For a long time, nobody knew quite what to say.

"Kelli's on her way," Andy whispered.

"And Steve?" Charlotte asked, her voice breaking.

"I haven't heard from him all day," Andy said. "I

texted Jonathon and Isabella, but neither of them has written back."

"They'll be here," Claire said, perhaps because she didn't know what else to say. "Where else would they be if not with her?" She eyed the coffin as though the woman inside could hear them speak.

Charlotte stepped closer to the coffin, her heart in her throat. "It's strange to think how long she's been in our lives."

"I've known her since I was a teenager," Andy muttered. "She used to come to my baseball games."

Charlotte's eyes welled with tears. "She gave me so much advice when I was pregnant with Rachel. I'll never forget when I had a breakdown in front of her. I told her I couldn't do it. She just laughed and said, 'If anyone can do it, a Montgomery woman can.' I understood, then, that she thought of our family as a strong and powerful family. She felt lucky to be with us." Charlotte wiped a tear from her cheek as she added, "I hope she knows how much we love her."

* * *

This is the story Charlotte had heard about the events of that fateful Tuesday.

Just as Laura had promised, she'd headed off the island to move Isabella into her room in a shared apartment in Brooklyn. Together, they'd driven Laura's car onto the ferry and leaped onto the top of the ferry to wave goodbye to the island Isabella held so dear. Afterward, they'd grabbed coffees, chatted about the logistics of the day, and then returned to Laura's vehicle to make the five-hour trek to NYC.

Once they'd arrived at the apartment, Laura and Isabella had carried Isabella's single suitcase and single backpack up the stairs, where Isabella's brand-new room-mate had greeted them. Together, Isabella and Laura had sat on the edge of Isabella's new (very used) mattress and bickered about buying new sheets. Isabella had maintained that she didn't need anything else, while Laura worried that the crummy sheets the previous tenant had left behind "just wouldn't do."

Ultimately, they'd decided to go grab a coffee at a nearby coffee shop. Once there, Laura began to press the bedsheet issue again. Isabella described the mood as "tense but hilarious," with Laura begging Isabella to let her mother set her up right. "It's your new life. I want it to be perfect," Laura had said. To this, Isabella had said, "There's no way it's going to be perfect! That's the point!"

It wasn't long after that that Laura dropped dead of a brain aneurysm.

She'd been declared dead at that very coffee shop, with Isabella screaming over top of her mother's body. It had taken Isabella a good two hours to get up the confidence to call her father back on the island. When she had, Steve had been hard at work, searching for Rachel. After that, his world crumbled.

* * *

"Is he here yet?" Kelli appeared at the funeral home a bit after Andy. She wore a sharply cut black dress with a high neckline but shoved her hands in her pockets nervously. This counteracted the "chicness" of the dress.

"Not yet. And he won't answer our calls," Andy said.

He stood on his creaking legs and hugged Kelli close. Kelli and Andy's relationship had always resembled Claire and Charlotte's. Who, Charlotte wondered now, had been closest to Steve? Perhaps that was the tragedy of having an odd number of siblings. Steve had never had his Claire. But it hadn't mattered, as he and Laura had been thicker than thieves.

Now, he was alone.

Charlotte and Claire finished propping the flowers on the coffin itself. The lilies were vibrant, arching wide open to reveal their long, white petals. Charlotte might have called them "too beautiful" for such a horrendous affair. But lilies were what you did for funerals. Everyone knew that.

Kelli propped her hands on her hips and assessed the floral decoration. "It looks really good, Claire," she said softly.

Claire stuttered. "I didn't know what to do. Maybe it's all too much."

Kelli shook her head. "It's just perfect."

Charlotte collapsed in the chair next to Andy and dropped her head on his shoulder. He smelled of coffee and baby cream; it was clear he had a newborn at home. Life and death; always seemed to come together.

"There he is." Claire spotted Steve hovering in the doorway, speaking softly with one of the funeral directors. When Charlotte turned to look, she discovered a shadow of a man, his shoulders arched forward and the wrinkles on his forehead deep.

He no longer looked like her strong and powerful older brother.

He looked destroyed.

Steve took his first step into the larger room, his eyes

on the coffin. Charlotte leaped to her feet, watching his every move. Slowly, he walked down the aisle, his elbows shifting against his suit jacket. In the past three days, he looked like he'd lost a bit of weight. If Charlotte had to guess, he probably hadn't eaten anything at all.

At the coffin, Steve splayed both of his hands over the wood, closed his eyes, and exhaled all the air from his lungs. Charlotte, Claire, Andy, and Kelli stepped forward to surround him. Charlotte placed her hand delicately on the top of his back. His sturdy heartbeat vibrated through his chest. How bizarre that Laura's heart had just stopped like that, without warning. No one was safe.

"Where are the kids?" Charlotte finally asked. She knew better than to say how sorry she was. Steve would hear that enough over the course of the next hours, days, weeks, and months.

"Isabella's in the car," Steve muttered. "And Jonathon's at the playground next door with his kids. They need to get out their energy before something like this."

Charlotte's throat was terribly tight. Andy inhaled a deep breath, preparing to say something. Before he could, one of the funeral directors ambled in and suggested, in a soft tone, that it was time for the coffin to be opened. Steve looked at him crossly for a long time before he nodded somberly and stepped back.

"It's time," he muttered, mostly to himself. "She wouldn't want to hide away. Not today."

Charlotte wasn't entirely sure what that meant, but she knew better than to mess around with his thought processes. He was grieving. There was no way around it.

Laura didn't look like herself. Nobody ever really did once they'd died. Charlotte had heard people say things like, "Oh, she looks so good. They did a good job," while at funerals. She'd always thought these comments were insensitive at best and cruel at worst. The fact of it was that Laura no longer lived in that body. She'd carried it around for the past forty-plus years— had gotten married in it, given birth in it, gone running and swimming and sailing in it. And then, one day, it had given up on her and sent her on her way.

Steve placed his hand on hers, there in the coffin, and knelt gently to whisper something to her. None of the other Montgomery siblings could hear exactly what he said.

"Dad?" Jonathon appeared at the back of the large room, one of his children in his arms. His cheeks were blotchy from tears.

Steve turned back and met his son in the center of the room. They exchanged more words. Charlotte and Andy locked eyes, both pale. Jonathon, too, looked hollowed out. Jonathon's child was dressed in black, his cheeks pink from playing on the playground. His hair was rugged and wild. Not long ago, Charlotte had witnessed Laura cradling this child, her grandchild. "I just love being a grandmother," she'd told Charlotte. "You get to love and squeeze them to no end. And then, when things get tough, you get to send them home."

Charlotte had laughed at that. When Laura had reminded her that one day, Rachel would probably give Charlotte grandchildren of her own, however, Charlotte had refuted this. Time couldn't possibly pass that quickly, she'd told herself at the time.

People began to arrive at four-thirty. Charlotte sat with her siblings, watching as Steve, Isabella, and Jonathon greeted the mourners as they ambled in. One after another, they lifted their hands for handshakes and bent their heads to hear whispered words of encouragement and sorrow. Isabella looked haggard, as though she'd aged ten years in four days.

"Do you think she'll go back to New York?" Claire whispered in Charlotte's ear.

Charlotte shook her head almost violently. "How could she? She took one step off the island, and the world proved itself to be a horrible and cruel place. I would be terrified."

Claire bit her lower lip. "I'd hate for her to feel like her life is over, now. I'd hate for her to live in fear. Maybe, when the time comes, we can find a way to help her heal and try to leave the island again. It's her dream."

Everett and Rachel entered the funeral home. Rachel wore one of Charlotte's simple black gowns. Its puffy sleeves shivered in the breeze from the front door. When she spotted Isabella, she stepped delicately forward and wrapped her arms around her older cousin. The pair had never been "close," exactly— a gap of five years was a lot as children. But nevertheless, Rachel had known Isabella since she'd been a child. She'd looked up to her. There was nothing worse than watching your heroes fall apart.

Everett shook Steve's hand and placed his left hand gently on Steve's shoulder. He said something that made Steve nod. He then shook Jonathon's hand and gave Isabella a hug. His face was shadowed, his head bent low.

Everett and Rachel slipped into the row behind Kelli, Andy, Charlotte, and Claire. Everett stepped up to kiss Charlotte on the cheek and whispered, "How are you doing?"

Charlotte lifted her shoulders. "Thank you for coming."

"Nowhere else I'd be," Everett told her firmly.

A strange voice in the back of Charlotte's head refuted this. Everett had found every reason to be on Orcas Island recently. After learning of Laura's death, he'd jumped on the next flight home, deciding to finish the article from Martha's Vineyard. But why hadn't that been a possibility beforehand? Why did he strive to live his life apart?

Was he bored of her?

Rachel hugged Charlotte from behind, whispering, "Gosh, I hope Isabella is okay."

Charlotte turned and locked eyes with her daughter. "You need to be there for her," she told her under her breath.

"I know."

What Charlotte meant was that Charlotte and Rachel had been through this before. They knew the ups and downs of grief; they understood the terror of losing someone you'd planned to have in your life forever. When Jason had died, they'd had no blueprint to follow. People had bought them books about grief; they'd gone to therapy; they'd read blogs. But despite their best efforts, they'd felt like they were drowning. Perhaps in many ways, it still felt like that.

The funeral began at five. The pastor of Oak Bluffs Presbyterian stood at the front of the collection of more than two hundred mourners and led them in prayer. No one, not even the little kids in attendance, made a single noise. It was eerie.

Afterward, the pastor spoke at length about Laura's commitment to her family and her love for the island of Martha's Vineyard. To Charlotte, the words seemed sterile. *Had this pastor been there for any of their family dinners? Had he been seated at Steve and Laura's wedding all those years ago, watching as they'd danced their first dance to "Wonderful Tonight" by Eric Clapton? Could he possibly understand the unique relationship that Laura had had with each of her children? No. The answer was no.*

After the pastor finished his final prayer, Isabella stood on quivering heels and walked toward the front. Slowly, she removed a letter from the pocket of her dress and unfolded it. When she spoke, she rasped into the microphone and then leaned her head back. Already, she seemed embarrassed.

And more than that, up there at the pulpit, she seemed to look especially like her mother. Charlotte had never noticed how similar they looked before. It was eerie.

"When I first started writing this speech," Isabella began, "I wrote a list of everything my mother had done for my brother, my father, and I. As you can imagine, the list was incredibly long. I wrote down everything I could think of— that she packed our lunches every day for school, that she drove me to and from every after-school activity, that she held us when we cried and fetched Band-Aids when we'd hurt ourselves and put gas in our cars and made our favorite meals when we were sad. But when my list got really, really long, I realized how wrong I'd been to even make it. Because yes, my mother was there for each of us in every conceivable way. But she was also her own person, with her own life."

Isabella's chin quivered. She inhaled sharply and flipped the small page over. Charlotte's heart nearly burst.

"My mother's name was Laura Miller Montgomery.

She was born forty-seven years ago and always said that she grew up a tomboy. The pictures prove that. She was always seen in a pair of overalls with scabbed knees and a big, goofy smile. Back then, and into her forties, she liked to run and run fast— and she even beat me at a mini-marathon a few years ago. I was eighteen years old and supposedly in the prime of my life, but Mom just whizzed past me like I was a pile of dust."

The mourners across the funeral home tittered with tearful laughter. Isabella began to struggle, her voice breaking.

"She embarrassed me. Oh gosh, she embarrassed me so much! She was always in the kitchen, dancing and singing to John Mellencamp and Hall & Oates. When my friends came over, I swear, she made a point to sing louder. But I couldn't exactly tell her to stop. I knew, even as a stupid teenage girl, that the amount of joy my mother had wasn't the kind you should stomp out."

Rachel placed her hand on Charlotte's shoulder and squeezed gently, a reminder of the love she had for her mother. Charlotte laced her fingers through Rachel's.

"I'll miss her," Isabella stuttered, swiping her hand across her left cheek. "I'll miss the way she talked and gossiped. I'll miss the silly text messages she sent me. I'll miss the way she opened all the windows in the morning and greeted a brand-new day. But most of all, I'll miss the love she had for me. She—" Here, Isabella closed her eyes tightly, overwhelmed. "She brought me to New York City on her final day. She told me the buildings were too tall, that people should never have dared to build anything so high up. She asked me if I would ever come back to Martha's Vineyard, and I told her that I wasn't sure. That I wanted to see what the world had to offer me. Mom said

I was braver than she ever was. But I don't think that's true. She was a live wire, unique and opinionated. She wore her heart on her sleeve. I hope as I get older, I become more and more like her. I hope I find a way to keep her alive."

Isabella's shoulders quivered and shook. She shoved the paper back in her pocket and placed her hand over her mouth to stifle a sob. After that, she rushed from the pulpit, down the aisle, and out into the foyer. This left a pocket of silence. No one knew what to do next.

Charlotte caught sight of Steve in the front row. His head was bent forward, his eyes toward his shoes. Only a few feet away, the love of his life lay back in her coffin with her hands folded gently over her stomach. There didn't seem to be a point to any of that suffering.

Chapter Fifteen

Regardless of the event, it seemed they always needed more ice. This seemed to be a fact of life and death. Charlotte hovered behind a long table at Steve's house, watching as mourners passed by, grabbing glasses of soda, juice, wine, and spirits. She beckoned for Everett, who chatted softly with Christine Sheridan in the corner. Everett hustled toward her, his face urgent. "Hey, honey, what can I get you?"

Charlotte leafed for her wallet. "Can you please go out and get two or three big bags of ice?"

Everett waved away her wallet. "Not a problem. Anything else?"

Charlotte eyed the long table. A large vegetable platter had been put out, along with a big pot of meatballs with gravy, Kerry's clam chowder, homemade biscuits and croissants, mini sandwiches, several types of cake and pie, and three different salads. Hungry mourners stood around Steve and Laura's house with their paper plates lifted as they nibbled and chatted.

"Claire?" Charlotte got Claire's attention, where she hovered in the doorway between the living room and the kitchen. She looked like a lost puppy.

"What's up?"

"Everett's headed out to get more ice," Charlotte said.

"Oh, thank God." Claire wiped her hands on a towel. All the color had drained from her cheeks.

"Do we need anything else?" Charlotte asked.

Claire bit her lip. "Maybe some fruit? Fresh fruit? We ran out of strawberries and blueberries about forty-five minutes ago."

"I'm on it," Everett said. He then cupped Charlotte's elbow and whispered in her ear, "I haven't seen you sit down in over two hours. Why don't you come with me? Take a rest in my car while I shop?"

Charlotte snapped her head left, then right. "They need me," she told him quietly.

"People can pour their own drinks," Everett told her firmly. "You need to take care of yourself, too."

But Everett couldn't possibly understand what this meant. Steve's wife had died so suddenly; she wasn't coming back. How many nights had Charlotte gaped at her front door, daring Jason to march back through it, stinking of fish from his long day of fishing? How many nights had she cried herself to sleep?

"I have to be here for Steve," she replied sharply. She wanted to add: *You just don't get it.* But she held her tongue.

Everett kissed her cheek gently and stepped out, his keys jangling as he walked. Charlotte listened to the soft creak and close of the front door. In a moment, Everett's motor whirred from the driveway.

In his absence, Lola Sheridan appeared in front of the food table. She wore a long black bohemian dress, and her hair flowed gorgeously down her back. Behind her, her daughter, Audrey, held her toddler in her arms as she spoke with her grandfather, Uncle Wes.

"Are you holding up, okay?" Lola asked softly.

Charlotte nodded. "I'm just doing all I can to help out." With a flourish, she removed an empty platter from the food table and beckoned for Lola to grab anything she wanted.

"This kind of tragedy, well," Lola continued, her eyes to the ground. "It terrifies me. I've held my daughter extra-close since it happened."

"Me too," Charlotte whispered.

"Steve looks..." Lola trailed off.

"I know," Charlotte breathed. With the empty plate in the crook of her arm, she added, "It's only going to get worse."

It was Lola's turn to become terribly pale. Her eyes flashed back toward Tommy Gasbarro, whom she'd only just married the previous June. It was her first marriage. Charlotte could practically read Lola's mind. Probably, she'd begun to fear for Tommy's life. What did it mean to fall in love and get married? It meant setting yourself up for a terrible future heartbreak. Inevitably, if everything worked out, you fell in love and that love lasted. One of you left the earth before the other. Inevitably, you wound up alone.

Charlotte knew that. She'd been left alone.

But she didn't have time for Lola's fears.

Everett returned with three bags of ice and enough strawberries, blueberries, blackberries, and raspberries to feed a small, berry-obsessed army. Charlotte cleaned the berries in the sink and placed them in a large china bowl. Everett watched her in the kitchen, wordless. In the next room, laughter erupted, which sounded so strange in the somber wake.

When Charlotte turned to take the berries out to the long table, Everett stepped between her and the doorway, his arms extended. Charlotte's heart banged loudly in her chest. She knew, instinctively, that Everett needed to feel like he was supporting her. He needed to hug her, kiss her, and be there for her. But something about Laura's death and Everett's newfound career out west made her cold. She stepped to the side of his hug, shaking her head.

"Baby," Everett whispered, his voice breaking.

"I just have to put these out," Charlotte said, blinking back tears. She hustled out and placed the china bowl delicately in the center of the table. Everett remained in the kitchen, lurking like a shadow. She'd hurt his feelings, but she didn't have space in her brain to think much more about it.

Charlotte wandered through the crowd, checking on empty plates and empty glasses. After refilling a gin and tonic and a glass of wine for two friends of Steve, she discovered Steve himself, seated on the couch in the living room. Isabella sat beside him, her hands cupping her knees. They stared forward, watching the television. They'd turned off the sound, and subtitles ran forward quickly, trying to keep up with the quick speech. It was just Martha's Vineyard's local news' station. On-screen, a young reporter stood in front of the Martha's Vineyard humane society, discussing a new batch of kittens. Both Steve and Isabella watched the segment as though the woman spoke about the future of the world.

"Can I get you two anything?" Charlotte heard herself ask.

Steve and Isabella glanced up, surprised that anyone was there. Probably, they'd forgotten that their house was filled with guests. Charlotte remembered that from the early days of Jason's death: distraction was key.

"Oh. Hi, Charlotte," Steve said.

"Aunt Charlotte, do you think I should adopt a kitten?" Isabella asked.

"Oh. Um." Charlotte furrowed her brow. "I don't know about that."

"Maybe I should," Isabella muttered to herself. "Mom always talked about it. I don't know why she never did?"

"The furniture," Steve said. "She was worried about the cat ruining the stupid furniture."

"Huh." Isabella gaped at him for a long moment.

It was true that preserving the furniture sounded like the stupidest thing in the world just then. You couldn't take furniture with you to heaven.

"I'll get you both something to drink. Isabella, you like wine, don't you? And Steve, a beer?" Charlotte heard herself ask. She so needed them to need something. She so needed to help them— perhaps in the same way Everett needed to help her.

It all seemed so useless.

Charlotte poured Isabella a glass of wine and grabbed Steve a beer from the fridge. After she dropped off the drinks, she turned to find Uncle Wes stationed in the center of the room. His skin was oddly gray and sallow. Charlotte made a mental note to ask Amanda or Audrey, his granddaughters and roommates, if he was eating well.

Were they all falling apart?

"Hello, Charlotte," Uncle Wes began, palming the back of his neck.

"Hi, Uncle Wes. Can I get you something to eat or drink?"

Wes shook his head. He then bent it low to whisper in her ear. "When I look at Steve, I see myself during those days, weeks, and months after Anna passed. I was just a lost puppy, too broken-hearted to live in the world."

Charlotte's eyes welled with tears. She could feel the tragedy behind Wes's words. The sorrow never really left.

"I know you know what that's like," Wes continued.

Charlotte locked eyes with her uncle. The air grew taut. It was remarkable, really, how "with it" Wes remained, despite his dementia diagnosis. "I'll be by his side through all of it," Charlotte promised. "There's nowhere else I'd rather be."

"You're stronger than most," Wes told her firmly. "Much stronger than I was back then."

"I don't know about that," Charlotte told him. "We all have our own ways of falling apart."

"I suppose you're right."

When Charlotte returned to the long table to refill and restock, she discovered Everett hard at work. He'd donned an apron and wrapped a loose strand of hair around his ear, speeding between the kitchen and the table to fetch fresh croissants, a new package of butter, more hummus, and three new bottles of wine.

"Thank you for coming," he said to a young woman as he refilled her glass of wine. "Laura was a remarkable woman. I feel so lucky to have known her, even for the brief time that I did."

Charlotte hovered behind the growing crowd as they

filled their plates and greeted Everett kindly. Everett hadn't yet noticed her. His smile was utterly kind and handsome, and he seemed to bring a sense of ease to the surroundings. Charlotte cursed herself for having thought that he couldn't possibly understand. *What did anyone actually understand about death, anyway?* He wanted to help out. That was enough.

When the crowd in front of the food table dissipated, Charlotte stepped around and fell into Everett. Silent tears slipped from her eyes, staining his shirt. His arms were powerful around her, holding her tightly against him as she shook. Slowly, he led her toward the kitchen, where they stood in silence, holding onto each other as a means of survival.

Charlotte finally lifted her eyes toward his and said, "I'm sorry I've been so distant."

Everett shook his head. "There's no blueprint for how to act." He traced a strand behind her ear and added, "I'm just so sorry I wasn't here when it happened."

Charlotte stuttered. "You can't plan for stuff like that. You have to keep living and living well. I know that."

"You know it better than most," Everett reminded her.

It was so nice to be seen, Charlotte thought. It was so nice that Everett allowed her to remember Jason and to live in her grief when it came. It was ultimate empathy.

"I'm so glad I get to marry you," Charlotte whispered.

"I'm the lucky one."

They kissed tenderly. Outside, another guest said, "Is there any more ice?" Charlotte chuckled, mid-kiss, as Everett called out, "I'm on my way with more!" Charlotte and Everett locked eyes just before Everett stepped back to gather the ice from the freezer. At the same time, they said, "I love you," then burst into anxious giggles.

"Jinx," Charlotte quipped. She felt dizzy with grief and laughter. There was no way to understand it. She could remember back to when Jason had died, laughing herself to bits with Claire until she'd fallen to her kitchen floor. When she'd come to, she hadn't been able to remember what had been so funny. Still, she'd been grateful for the moments of laughter; they'd allowed her to forget her pain.

* * *

That night, after everyone had departed for the night, Charlotte, Claire, and Kelli remained in the kitchen for the final clean-up. Already, Isabella had locked herself in her bedroom, taking multiple bags of snacks along with her. Jonathon and his wife had taken their children back home, both bleary-eyed and exhausted.

This left only Steve downstairs, still on the couch. His eyes were void of any emotion as he stared off into space. In the kitchen, Charlotte, Claire, and Kelli whispered about what to do.

"I just worry that he won't be able to sleep," Claire confessed as she dried a dish and placed it delicately in a cabinet.

"I don't think he's slept since it happened," Kelli offered.

"I brought some melatonin," Charlotte said. "But I think he needs something stronger."

Kelli swiped a rag across the counter, shaking her head. In the next room, Steve flicked through the channels and raised the volume so that it became a storm of sound. Charlotte exhaled all the air from her lungs and said, finally, "I want to go talk to him."

"Do you know what you'll say?" Claire asked softly.

Charlotte shook her head. "Not at all. All these memories keep coming up of those first few days after Jason died. Maybe I can just make him feel less alone?"

Claire and Kelli nodded, their eyes widening. Before Charlotte lost her nerve, she turned on her heel and headed back toward the living room. There, Steve sat with his knees wide open and his shoulders hunched. For the first time, perhaps ever, Charlotte saw their father in Steve's stance— the older version.

One day, they would all be so old. God willing, of course.

"Hi, honey." Charlotte sat at the far edge of the couch, not wanting to encroach on his space. She rubbed her knees nervously and eyed the television, where Steve had turned on a show about open-water fishing. She flinched. Jason had been a fisherman.

"Oh. Gosh, Charlotte. What am I doing?" Steve remembered himself, grabbing the remote and flicking around before he landed on *The Shawshank Redemption*. But a split-second later, the characters onscreen began to discuss the issue of the main character killing his wife.

"He didn't do it," Steve muttered, remembering the plot. "God. Can you imagine? Going through the grief of losing the one you love the most and then being accused of murdering her?"

Charlotte dropped her chin. The film was powerful, sometimes overwhelming. It seemed like it was always on TV, appearing on one station or another. Given the content, Charlotte thought it appeared almost too much.

147

It was a constant reminder of the people and time you lost along the way.

"Steve," Charlotte began. "I just want to tell you that you can talk to me. About any of it."

Steve grabbed the remote and lowered the volume. His brow furrowed, then he rasped, "I can't believe you went through this already. This is the greatest pain I've ever known."

Charlotte opened her lips to speak, but nothing came out.

"I'm so ashamed, Charlotte," Steve said, running his fingers through his hair. "I'm so ashamed of how happy I was when you met Everett. I thought to myself, 'Finally, she can be happy again.' How naive I was! Now, I understand. You've found happiness in spite of your sorrow. Because it never goes away, does it?"

Charlotte blinked back tears and slowly shook her head. "It never goes away." She couldn't lie to him. Not now.

Steve nodded his eyes to the television. "I keep replaying the last few moments I saw her alive. I walked her and Isabella to the car outside. Isabella was impatient; she thought they were going to miss the ferry. Laura was anxious, alternating between crying and making Isabella crazy with her worrying. I tried to keep the two of them calm with a few 'dad jokes' here and there. It worked, mostly."

Charlotte shivered with laughter. A small smile played across Steve's lips.

"I kissed her through the car window," Steve whispered. "It was just like any other goodbye. I barely noticed it at all. After that, I waved as she reversed down the driveway and headed off toward the ferry."

Steve's eyes were glassy with tears. "I wonder how many times I've kissed her goodbye. Thousands? Millions? We've been together for over twenty years. The math of that is ridiculous. I don't even want to do it."

Charlotte reached out a hand and placed it on Steve's. It was terribly cold, as though he'd been outside. She wanted to make him a plate of meatballs and fresh bread and demand that he eat. But she couldn't very well spoon-feed him, could she?

Finally, Steve's eyes flickered toward Charlotte's. After a long, dramatic pause, he whispered, "Just tell me how to get through this first week."

Charlotte's heart banged against her ribcage. "The first week is like being on fire. You're looking for signs of oxygen everywhere. There's smoke in every direction. The pain is so great that you can barely hear yourself think."

Steve nodded ever-so-slightly. "That's exactly right."

"But a little while later, the grief is like being under-water," Charlotte continued, her voice catching. "You're going through the motions, swimming forward through time. When people speak to you, their voices are muffled — just like when we tried to talk to each other underwater as kids."

Steve's cheek twitched. *Did he remember those long-ago days when they'd done that?* She could remember diving under the waves of the Vineyard Sound and listening hard as Claire screamed at her through the water. They'd done it for hours until they'd lost their voices.

"And later..." Charlotte began.

But Steve held up a hand. After a long pause, he said, "I'll get to later when I get to later. For now, I'll just prepare for this— the fire, then the water." He locked eyes with Charlotte's as he added a soft, "Thank you."

Charlotte squeezed his hand harder. "If you need anything at all..."

"I know who to call."

On television, *The Shawshank Redemption* returned from a commercial break. Andy Dufresne lifted his eyes toward the gorgeous blue of the sky above and dreamed of a future, one where he was free.

Chapter Sixteen

Wes splayed his diary across his lap and lifted his pen. For the first time in several days, he tried to scribe the events of the previous week. He felt he owed it to his family to remember, even if he so desperately wanted to forget.

But what day was it? He blinked toward the ceiling of his bedroom, listening to the soft music that Audrey played in the living room next door. Max babbled along with it as though he knew every word. Finally, he turned his head to inspect the calendar that hung over his dresser.

It was September 14, a Wednesday.

Already, Laura Montgomery had been deceased for eight days.

And Wes had hardly written a word about it.

September 14, 2022,

I was out with Susan on the evening of Tuesday, September 6th. My niece Charlotte's daughter, Rachel, was missing, and everyone in the family was hard at work looking for her.

I still don't know where she'd run off to. Rumor has it she struggles in high school and needed to "get away." As a sixty-nine-year-old man, I can certainly understand the desire for privacy. Now that I have dementia, it seems that people give me privacy less and less.

But I digress. This isn't about me.

As Susan and I returned to the Sunrise Cove to search again for Rachel along the waterline, she received a call from Charlotte. Susan asked Charlotte to calm down so that she could understand what she was saying. Susan then said something like, "Oh no. Oh no. Oh my God." She was white as a sheet. When she got off the phone, she told me that my nephew, Steve, had lost his wife, Laura. She died of a brain aneurysm down in New York City.

As an aging man, I have a complicated relationship with death. On the one hand, I often think I'm ready for it. I've lived a prosperous life. I have three wonderful daughters and beautiful grandchildren. I even have a great-grandchild whose middle name is my first name.

On the other hand, the darkness of that eternal fate terrifies me. One minute, Laura was here, offering her love and support to Steve and the rest of our family. The next, she was gone.

Charlotte, Claire, and Kelli pitched in for the wake. It was strange to watch them running about like that, taking care of the family the way Anna and Kerry used to, together. My girls were there as well, helping when they could. Mostly, Charlotte and Claire kicked them out of the kitchen, saying they didn't need any help. My best guess is that they wanted to break down in private. Extended family is still family— but it's just not the same. There are secrets you still keep from one another.

Wes heaved a sigh, tapping his pen along the outer

edge of the page. He was proud of himself, in a sense, for having written at all. For too long, he'd allowed his thoughts to flow around in the back of his mind without rhyme or reason. He felt better when he pinned them down.

He went on:

In my own humble existence, I must confess that I've felt terribly sad. It feels selfish to say so, especially when my nephew Steve has experienced so much loss.

But in short, my dear friend, Beatrice, has hardly reached out since that strange evening at the Birdwatching Convention. I watched her fall in love with that handsome man from the Midwest. As my tongue wilted in my mouth, he captivated her. That's the sort of man Beatrice deserves. Not me.

Since then, I've hardly gone birdwatching myself. Kellan is away, and my binoculars hang on the wall, waiting for me. Right now, all birds remind me of her and of the hope I once had for our future. I know that will pass one day. For now, I'll stew in my own sorrows.

Suddenly, a knock rang out at Wes's bedroom door. He shoved the diary beneath the comforter on his bed and called, "Come in!" For whatever reason, the idea of his granddaughters discovering his private thoughts mortified him. He was like a teenager in that respect.

Audrey appeared in the crack of the door with a big wooden spoon lifted. Her smile was infectious. "Hi, Grandpa!"

Wes made his best effort to sound surprised. "Hi, there! What are you up to?"

"Amanda just got home," Audrey explained, waving the wooden spoon behind her. "And we were wondering if you wanted to go for a walk?"

Amanda appeared behind Audrey with little Max lifted against her. Her smile was just as big, and her engagement ring sparkled on her fourth finger. "It's a gorgeous day, Grandpa."

Had his granddaughters been worried about him? It was possible. They were pretty perceptive.

"You two should go on without me," Wes told them. He wanted to get back to his diary.

"Grandpa, please?" Audrey pleaded, half-whining. "Max says he won't go without you. Will you, Max?"

It was too easy to manipulate a man as full of love as Wes Sheridan. Before long, he found himself with his tennis shoes on and his hands shoved in his jean pockets as he walked alongside his granddaughters. The temperature was in the sixties, his favorite, and the waves were sea-foam green and foggy beneath the gray sky.

"What have you been up to, Grandpa?" Amanda asked him, lacing her arm through his.

Wes stuttered, searching his mind for something to say that had nothing to do with Beatrice and his broken heart.

"I've been reading a lot," he lied.

"Oh! What have you been reading?" Amanda asked.

Wes searched his mind for the memory of a single book title. There were millions of books; he just needed one title!

"Um. That guy? Who writes about the law?"

"James Patterson!" Audrey recited.

"That's the one," Wes affirmed, although he hadn't read a James Patterson book in over ten years.

Amanda began to chatter about a book she'd read that week. Max, who wiggled madly in Audrey's arms, was placed on the sand, where he rushed forward on wobbly legs. Wes hardly heard a word Amanda said. Before he knew what had happened, however, he heard himself agreeing to head to the Sunrise Cove.

"Sam's there right now," Amanda explained as they walked toward the path that would lead them there. "He says the lunch special today is exquisite."

"Sam uses the word 'exquisite'?" Audrey quipped.

Amanda rolled her eyes. "Sam has an excellent vocabulary."

"Sam sounds very pretentious," Audrey teased. "I can't wait to tease him about this when we get there. Exquisite! Seriously?" She cackled, lifting Max back into her arms.

En route to the Sunrise Cove, Amanda jumped on a call with Susan, inviting her to meet them for lunch. It occurred to Wes that normally, Amanda was at the law office during the week. He forced himself to ask why she wasn't there. To this, Amanda waved a hand and said, "We're low on cases this week for the first time in months, so I'm doing more work from home. On top of it all, I have some online classes to finish. Sometimes, Mom forgets that I'm still a law student."

"Oh. That's right," Wes said, although he, too, had forgotten. *How many other things about his family had he forgotten?* It terrified him to know.

When they entered the Sunrise Cove, Amanda traipsed forward and kissed Sam directly on the mouth. (Wes had been too terrified to kiss his girlfriend in front of his own parents back in the old days, let alone his grandparents. Times had certainly changed.)

"Hi, Mr. Sheridan!" Sam greeted him. "And Audrey and Max."

Max squealed and cried, "Sam!" Sam laughed and

reached out to grab Max's hand, wiggling it back and forth. Very soon, Wes could tell, Amanda and Sam would have a little baby of their own.

Now for the first time, Wes wondered what Beatrice felt about never having been a mother. *Did she regret it? Or had it been purposeful so that she could commit herself fully to her career?* Why hadn't Wes asked her these pertinent questions? Had she thought that he hadn't cared about her? Had she thought him to be selfish and cruel?

"Hello, hello! Look what the cat dragged in!" Susan and Lola stepped out of the Bistro. Lola was sun-tanned, her long legs protruding from a short skirt. Susan wore her law office garb, a suit jacket, and a long pair of slacks. Both were stunning. Wes's heart swelled with pride.

Lola hugged Wes and said, "Did the girls drag you out of the house?"

Wes's stomach tightened. *Had Audrey told Lola that he'd been spending too much time in his bedroom?* "You know that I get out and about," he said.

"Oh, I know that," Lola replied. She lowered her voice to add, "It's been a hard week on all of us. I haven't known what to do with myself."

Wes grimaced as they walked back toward the Bistro. "Have you seen Steve?"

"I think Charlotte is keeping tabs on him," Lola affirmed as she lifted a hand to wave to Zach. He waved back before ducking into the steam of the Bistro kitchen.

"They have to take care of each other," Wes repeated. "I hope Steve knows that he has a home with us, too."

But already, Audrey leaped forward to chat with her mother about something related to Max. Lola fell into a steady rhythm with her only child as Max babbled, his eyes locked onto Wes. Wes waved a hand at his great-grandchild, making peace with being ignored.

Lunch went on like that. Wes sat at the table with Lola, Susan, Audrey, Amanda, and Max, who was up in a highchair, a bib around his neck. The Sheridan women wanted to avoid talking about Laura Montgomery; enough had been said. But this led them to topics that Wes had very little understanding of. Namely, there was non-stop talk about Amanda's upcoming wedding to Sam.

Wes chewed at the end of his sandwich. It was hard for him to remember the last time he'd ever been hungry. He gaped at the interior of the sandwich, which was ham and cheese and some unrecognizable sauce. Had his mother ever tasted that sauce, she would have said, *"What the heck have you done to this sandwich?"* It seemed that everyone wanted to "dress up" everything on the menu these days. Classics were no longer accepted.

It was no longer his time.

Gosh, his heart hurt. He bent his head forward and placed his sandwich back on the plate. His daughters and granddaughters seemed not to notice. He forced himself to drink some water and breathe deeply: inhale, exhale. Inhale, exhale. Still, his thoughts raced.

Always, his thoughts returned to Beatrice.

What had he done wrong?

Would he ever see her again?

Did she know that she'd been his bright light in an otherwise darkening reality?

He should have told her. Life was far too short not to tell people what was on your mind. Love was everything. The love for Laura would remain in Steve's heart forever, just as Wes's love for Anna would go on into eternity.

Suddenly, Wes leaped to his feet. The chair teetered

behind him, finally drawing attention from Susan and Lola.

"Dad, are you all right?" Lola asked.

"Oh, I'm fine," Wes replied, trying on a smile. "I just have to run to the restroom."

"Okay!" Lola gave him her beautiful smile and then returned her gaze to Amanda, who spoke about wedding cakes as though they were the secret to solving all the world's problems.

Wes marched with purpose down the Bistro hallway. His fingers fluttered across his pockets, taking stock of what he had on him. His wallet, thankfully. His phone. Unfortunately, he'd left his diary under the comforter on his bed. He would have to make do without it.

Sam was busy with a new Sunrise Cove patron, which allowed Wes to slip easily into the soft light of the Wednesday afternoon. He walked easily toward the street, his hands in his pockets. If he shifted his perception just so, he could imagine himself as a much younger man— in his twenties, maybe. Anna was just inside, balancing the checkbook. His children were babies or toddlers. His entire life was ahead of him— heartache included.

What a magical thing it would be to go back and see it all happen again. He would appreciate it better this time. How ignorant he'd been at the time, thinking it would all last forever.

Nothing lasted. Nothing.

Along Main Street, Wes hailed a taxi. It wasn't something he was accustomed to doing; it was just something he'd seen in movies and TV shows. Still, it seemed simple enough, perhaps too simple. The taxi driver asked him where he wanted to go, and, after a moment's hesitation,

Wes said, "I'd like to go to the Katama Lodge and Wellness Spa. Please."

The driver replied, "Sounds good to me!" He then smacked the meter, which recorded how far they'd traveled and how much money he'd earned. Wes buckled his seatbelt and cozied up in the back, his eyes on the world around him. The driver played a hip-hop radio station, one that Audrey probably would have loved. Wes bobbed his head around, wanting the taxi driver to think that he knew more about the modern world of music than he actually did.

"Beautiful day," the taxi driver said from the front seat.

"You got that right."

"What have you been up to today?" the driver asked.

Wes dropped his head against the headrest. The question rang through him, overwhelming him. *What had he been up to that day?*

"Oh. Not much," he returned, although it suddenly seemed that he'd been up to a lot. He dug through his mind, searching for a tidbit from his day. Anything. *What had he eaten? Had he gone birdwatching? What?*

"Sounds like a pretty good Wednesday to me," the driver quipped.

Wes reached to his side, hunting for his backpack, which so often held his diary. Nothing was there; it was empty. Had he forgotten his backpack somewhere? Where was his diary?

Come to think of it— where in the heck was he headed?

Wes's tongue became like sandpaper. He needed a sip of water so desperately. He tugged at his hair and gaped at the man who drove the car directly in front of him.

There was a little box beside him, upon which glowing numbers grew higher and higher. What did the numbers mean?

He gazed outside the window, watching the outskirts of Oak Bluffs evolve into Edgartown. He would have known this view, no matter what. *But why was he going to Edgartown? Who was this man?*

"Don't you just love autumn on the Vineyard?" the driver said, interrupting the silent panicking in Wes's head.

The Vineyard. Autumn. These were things Wes understood. He brightened, grateful to cling to something that seemed never to change.

"I just love it," Wes told him, dropping his head back on the headrest. A part of him demanded that he ask this kind young man where on earth they were headed. Another part told him not to do it. Doing so would reveal him as an "old and confused man."

If only he hadn't left his diary at home.

He knew better. He had a system! He always wrote everything down.

At a stoplight outside of Edgartown, a crow buzzed over them and clamped itself to the top of a stop sign. Wes barked with laughter. It was such an ominous sign. He longed to tell someone about it but couldn't imagine that anyone in his life cared about birds as much as he did. He kept the sentiment to himself.

Maybe it was a sign of his own doom. He would soon find out.

Chapter Seventeen

EVERETT: I'm around the corner. Headed your way.

Charlotte sat with her leg swinging on the bench outside the Oak Bluffs Ice Creamery. It was just past one-thirty, and Everett and Charlotte had agreed to meet for a late lunch snack between meetings. It had been a long time since they'd done anything so frivolous and "childish," like grab ice cream cones.

Charlotte practically jumped to her feet when she spotted him. As usual, he was handsome in his black pair of jeans and his black V-neck t-shirt. His dark hair cascaded past his ears, and his eyes were alert and expectant, looking at her as though she was the only woman in the world. Charlotte had to pinch herself. This man had actually asked her to marry him. This man was supposedly her "happily ever after."

When he reached her, Everett dipped her and kissed her so that Charlotte shrieked with laughter.

"Aren't you a Casanova?"

Everett tapped his nose against hers. "It's just good to see you."

Charlotte kissed him again and laced her arm through his. "You have a good morning of editing?"

"Can you tell?"

Charlotte laughed. He was always in a good mood when he had a successful workday. Everything in his professional life was exploding, in a good way. Charlotte willed herself to ride his happiness coattails, but it was easier said than done.

They headed inside the ice cream place, where Everett greeted the twenty-something worker warmly. He ordered a double chocolate cone, while Charlotte went with the mint chocolate chip. Everett tipped the ice cream worker with a five-dollar bill. Charlotte could have kissed him all over again but didn't want to embarrass the worker. She just adored it when he showed the depths of his generosity.

Back outside, Charlotte and Everett wandered toward the water, licking their cones. As Everett discussed his recent article, Charlotte allowed herself a brief reprieve from thinking about Laura and Steve. Happiness, she knew, was a trick of the mind.

When they reached the waterline, a long line of mint chocolate chip dribbled across Charlotte's hand. She laughed as Everett dabbed at it with his napkin, then bent to kiss her hand. Again, her heart lifted.

"Hey," she said suddenly, pressing her palm against his chest. "I'm sorry I was so distant last week."

Everett shook his head, his smile falling. There was a strange moment of silence. Charlotte's heart pounded in her ears.

"I was gone so much, Char," Everett murmured. "I feel so guilty about it."

"You shouldn't," she insisted.

"But I do." His eyes flashed. He took another lick from his ice cream cone and puckered his lips. "I just got off the phone with my editor."

Oh no, Charlotte thought. *Don't take him away again. Please. I need him here. We're building so much. Together.*

"What did he say?" Charlotte breathed, trying to sound neutral.

"He said that my stories have been a huge hit," Everett said, his eyes locking with hers.

"I'm not surprised," Charlotte returned. "You're so talented. The world is lucky to read your words and see your photographs."

Everett sighed. "Thank you for saying that." After another pause, he added, "The magazine wants more from me. More than I can probably give."

Charlotte arched her brow. "What do you mean?"

"The editor asked that I do a series of stories, all based in the northwest. Orcas Island and the others in the area. They want me to continue on with the same research that I've been conducting, digging into the restaurant and tourism industry, and even interviewing the locals."

Charlotte's heart fluttered like a bird. "Wow."

Everett nodded. "They want me to write as their expert in the area."

"Expert," Charlotte repeated, as though the word was foreign to her.

"Yeah." Everett's eyes grew clouded. His hand was covered in double-chocolate ice cream. He tossed it in the nearby trashcan and cleaned his hand as best as he could.

"That would mean more time in the northwest," Charlotte repeated. "A lot more time."

Everett could hardly look at her. His napkin was sticky with ice cream. Charlotte tossed the rest of her mint chocolate chip ice cream in the nearby trash can and dropped her shoulders. *What kind of woman was she, not being excited about her partner's professional success? She felt like a traitor.*

"I don't have to take it," Everett murmured.

Charlotte closed her eyes as tightly as she could. Already, a headache rang across her skull. Unfortunately, when she closed her eyes, two images popped to the surface: Laura in her coffin. Then, she was met with Jason in his.

"You have to go," Charlotte breathed. "You cannot say no to an opportunity like that."

Everett gaped at her. He looked at her as though she hadn't spoken English.

"Charlotte..." he tried.

Charlotte shook her head and turned away. She couldn't look at him, even as she pushed him further away. "I'm so proud of you," she breathed, her voice breaking. "I always knew you could do this."

Everett's large hand found her shoulder. His thumb kneaded her stiff muscles. After a long pause, he whispered words that seemed absolutely insane to her. "Would you ever consider going there with me? Full time?"

Charlotte whirled around, locking eyes with his. One hundred images burned through her mind— Lola and Jason on the boat the first night she and Jason ever kissed; Rachel, taking her first steps on the beach; moonrises and sunsets and countless hikes across the cliffs of Chilmark. Martha's Vineyard was her home; she'd never known another.

"I know. It's hard to think about," Everett said softly.

Charlotte whipped a hand toward the sailboats across the harbor. Stuttering, she said, "Have you even seen where we live?" She felt like a crazy person.

Everett laughed quietly. He had a small dot of ice cream on his lower lip. Charlotte ached to kiss it off but held herself back.

"We live in paradise," Everett whispered. "But don't you remember Orcas Island?"

Charlotte bit her lower lip, remembering. That week with Everett on Orcas Island had felt like a rebirth. Together, they'd scoured an impossibly beautiful island, chatted with strangers, eaten delectable food, and learned more about one another than ever before. The memory of the tragedy that had defined Charlotte's life had lurked in the back alleys of Charlotte's mind, giving her a break for once.

It had felt like starting over.

"I have to be here. For Rachel—"

"Her senior year. I know," Everett offered.

"And for St—"

"Steve. I know," Everett continued. His voice was heavy with empathy. "Steve cannot make it through these first few months without you. And you would never in a million years miss Rachel's senior year."

"Never," Charlotte echoed.

"But after that?" Everett repeated. "I don't mean to pressure you, Charlotte. I just know that we have something special here. Something that we should protect. I want to take this job, and I want you to follow me when you can because I love you more than I can possibly say. You know that, don't you?"

* * *

Later, after Everett had returned home to attend to another aspect of his burgeoning travel journalism career, Charlotte found herself with yet another bride who seemed overly willing to complain about all aspects of her wedding. This time, Charlotte wasn't patient, not in the least.

"I just don't think people are going to respect me as a bride if I don't have at least seven bridesmaids," the bride told her pointedly, sticking out her lower lip.

The bride's mother, who sat beside her with her ankles crossed, nodded along. "All the weddings we've gone to this year featured at least seven bridesmaids. Some had ten."

Charlotte gaped at them. *Had they forgotten the importance of what they'd begun to plan? Had they forgotten about the core fact of it— that the bride and groom were in love?*

How she wanted to scream at the bride, especially when she began to pout about the cupcake options the baker in town had. How she wanted to yell, *"You're in love! Don't you understand? It's the most beautiful thing in the world. Why aren't you more grateful for what you have?"*

But instead, she nodded along primly with the bride in question and jotted notes to herself. It was up to Charlotte to make this an unforgettable wedding experience.

Meanwhile, Everett would start a brand-new life out west without her.

Yet again, her heart would crack in two. But she could get through it better this time. She'd had so many years of practice.

Chapter Eighteen

The taxi pulled into a driveway on the southeastern edge of the island. Out front, a large sign read: KATAMA LOGDE AND WELLNESS SPA. Wes placed the tips of his fingers on the window and peered up at the gorgeous, wooden lodge — a place that seemed taken from a dream. *Had he seen it before?* He was vaguely sure he had.

"Here we are!" the driver of his cab announced and turned back to smile at Wes.

Wes felt very small, like a little kid on the bus to elementary school for the first time. The driver read the number from the little rectangle next to the steering wheel and blinked at Wes expectantly until Wes got the hint that that number was related to money. He grabbed his wallet from his back pocket and stared into it. He had a number of twenties, tens, and fives. He passed the expected amount across the seats and watched as the driver counted it out and slipped it into his own wallet.

Wes burned with questions. *Why was he at the Katama Lodge? Why had the driver taken him there? Was he far from home?* Instead, he smiled at the driver and opened the back door, stepping out into the cool air.

"Thanks a bunch," Wes heard himself say.

"Take care!" the driver said back.

Wes stood out on the lawn and watched as the cab backed out of the driveway and eased onto the main road. He lifted a hand to wave goodbye, but the driver didn't glance back.

Wes turned and gazed up at the Katama Lodge and Wellness Lodge. His brow furrowed as he caught sight of the glittering Katama Bay just beyond. As usual, the water around Martha's Vineyard calmed him. He stepped toward that water with his chin lifted as the sea winds breezed across his face.

Again, he willed himself to remember why on earth he was there. When he opened his eyes again, he found himself at the top of the hill that overlooked the gorgeous private beaches. Something told him that the residents of the Katama Lodge used those beaches. *Where had he learned that? Did everyone know that?*

He'd been called to this Lodge. This was a fact. He drew his fingers through his thinning hair and forced himself back toward the front door, closer to the sign on the lawn. After a dramatic breath, he shoved the door open and stood in the soft light of the foyer. Light rock music played from a speaker in the corner. The air smelled fresh and purified; it was almost medicinal. He closed his eyes as the door closed behind him.

Something about this space made him breathe deeper. It gave him a sense of the world, even if he hadn't a clue why he was there.

"Can I help you?" A voice rang out from the front desk. Wes opened his eyes to discover a woman in her thirties or forties, seated with a smile on her face. In front of her, a name card on the desk read: TERESA.

"Hello!" Wes recognized his voice and was grateful that he sounded friendly. This was the version of himself he knew best. He stepped closer to the desk, shaking his head. "My name is Wes Sheridan."

At least he knew that for sure.

Teresa's smile was unwavering. "Hi, Wes Sheridan. Do you have an appointment with us today?"

Wes clapped his hands. "That is a good question. Could you check for me on that computer of yours?"

Still, Teresa hardly batted an eye at his confusion. She was a saint. She placed her fingers on the keys and began to type furiously. Wes had never managed to type so quickly, not in all his years of using the computer. She then lifted her eyes and continued to smile as she said, "I'm terribly sorry, Wes Sheridan, but I don't seem to have an appointment for you on my computer. Would you like to make one?"

Wes's smile fell from his face. He blinked at the floor, despondent. He'd never needed his dang diary more than he did just then.

"Are you all right?" Teresa asked. She stood from her desk, her forehead wrinkled with worry. "Would you like me to get you a glass of water?"

Suddenly, the door behind the front desk opened to reveal another woman in her forties. She was bright-eyed and confident, her hair pulled half-up and the rest of her curls spilling across her shoulders.

"Hello, there. Welcome to the Katama Lodge," she said brightly.

"Hello!" Wes replied

"This is Wes Sheridan," Teresa announced, her eyes

widening. "He thought he might have an appointment today?"

The woman stepped closer, her smile waning just the slightest bit. "Hello, Wes. My name is Elsa Remington. You were friendly with my father. Maybe you remember him? Neal Remington?"

Wes was struck with an image of a middle-aged man with a smile not unlike this younger woman's. Slowly, the image became stronger.

"Neal. Of course," Wes returned as he snapped his finger against his temple. "We were both in the hospitality business."

"That's right," Elsa Remington said, her smile returning. "He always respected the way you did business."

"And I respected him," Wes affirmed proudly. "It was a good thing we did different things— him dealing with healing and natural medicine, and me, dealing strictly in the easy stuff. Restaurants and beds." Wes chortled as Elsa's smile widened.

Wes was rambling; he could feel it. Still, he had this sense that if he kept talking, he would eventually come to a conclusion about why in the heck he was at the Katama Lodge in the first place.

Finally, Elsa asked him. "So, Wes. To what do we owe the pleasure?"

Wes's smile fell to the floor. "I wish I could tell you that, Elsa." He blinked back tears, fearful all over again. If he wasn't mistaken, Elsa's father was now dead. Truly, he hadn't been that old. Perhaps Wes was next. Perhaps when Wes did die, he wouldn't remember a thing about his life. That terrified him most of all.

"Let's go get a smoothie together," Elsa said suddenly. "We have the most amazing smoothies on the island."

Wes cocked his head. "That sounds like something my granddaughter would make me. She's always telling me that I need more brain food."

"We all need more brainfood, Wes," Elsa said with a laugh. "Come on. I insist. I need an afternoon snack."

"Well. If you insist," Wes smiled.

* * *

Elsa showed Wes how to select the ingredients for his green smoothie. He opted for spinach, blueberries, chia seeds, and mangoes, all of which were tossed into a blender and whirred up into green gunk. Wes laughed. "It looks like the stuff in the lawnmower after mowing."

"You sound just like my father," Elsa told him as she selected her own ingredients. "But he eventually bought into all of this stuff. He wouldn't go a day without a green smoothie."

Wes wanted to ask why Neal had died, especially since he'd been so health conscious. But instead, he sipped his green smoothie and gazed out the mighty two-story windows that overlooked Katama Bay. Elsa explained that they'd blocked the windows from last year's hurricane. "The glass didn't break. It was a miracle," she said.

Wes and Elsa sat at the table with the best view of the bay. Behind them, women dressed in thick robes walked in sandals to grab their own green smoothies. Elsa explained that women from across the world came to the Lodge to heal. "Often, they've been traumatized. They've gone through divorce, or they've experienced a death in the family, or—"

"Or they've just gone through life, like the rest of us. With all the horrors that includes," Wes finished.

Elsa nodded knowingly. "You've gone through your own dark times, Wes. I know that."

"I suppose the whole island knows that," Wes said. He dropped his lips over his paper straw and sucked some green juice over his tongue. It was vaguely bitter with a hint of sweetness from the mangoes and blueberries.

"There's no escaping our stories on this island," Elsa agreed. "I've felt surrounded by death since I was a teenager.

Wes held the silence. He spread his hands out before him, showing the whites of his palms that hadn't gotten a hint of tan throughout the summer.

Suddenly, he found himself saying, "I don't know why I'm here. I normally keep a very diligent diary. I write down what I plan to do and what I've already done. That way, this stupid dementia doesn't get in my way."

Elsa scowled. "You sound really organized."

"I left my diary at home," Wes sputtered. "I couldn't be angrier with myself if I tried."

Elsa placed a hand on his upper arm. Wes was embarrassed by that arm, as it had previously been heavy with muscle. Now, it was mostly just bone.

"You made your way here for a reason. You're safe here. You must know that, somewhere inside of you," Elsa told him softly.

Wes's eyes filled with tears. "I hate this. I hate living with this messed-up brain."

Suddenly, a voice rang out from the opposite end of the great dining hall.

"Wes? Is that you?"

Wes rose up to lock eyes with an angel. There, wearing a navy-blue button-up dress, a pair of flats, and a soft cashmere cardigan, stood Beatrice Cunningham. Her blue eyes glittered with tears, and her lips were parted with surprise. She took a delicate step forward and touched her hair.

"Beatrice!" Wes rasped.

Elsa stood and turned to greet Beatrice. She was wordless.

Wes closed the distance between himself and Beatrice. Suddenly, everything became crystal clear. He'd jumped into that taxi on Main Street so that he could tell Beatrice how he felt— that he couldn't possibly live without her.

He placed his chin on her shoulder and shook as they hugged.

Beatrice murmured, "You're okay. You're okay, here," over and over again. If Wes wasn't mistaken, it sounded like she was crying.

Beatrice led Wes to her upstairs office. It was small and quaint, with a dark green couch pressed up beneath a large window and a mahogany desk covered in files and papers. Beatrice pressed a CD into a CD player, explaining that she still hadn't gotten the hang of "streaming websites" or whatever they were called. Wes waved it away and said, "I still prefer records." Beatrice laughed that gorgeous laugh of hers.

For a moment, everything seemed perfect.

But as Simon and Garfunkel sang out from her speaker, Beatrice placed her chin on her fist and said, "Wes, why are you here?"

Wes's voice broke with sorrow. "I haven't seen you in so long, Beatrice. Where have you been?"

For a long time, the only sound belonged to Simon

and Garfunkel. They sang "The Sound of Silence," which seemed too fitting for the moment. Hurriedly, Beatrice lifted a finger and changed the song to play "Old Friends."

"You ran out on me," Beatrice said suddenly. Her words weren't accusatory; they were simply fact.

Wes arched his brow. "What are you talking about?"

"At the birdwatching dinner," Beatrice continued. "We were all seated, eating and drinking together. I thought you went off to the bathroom, and then suddenly, you were gone. Nobody had any idea of where you'd gone. "

Beatrice's eyes were thick with tears. It seemed she had the ability to keep them in; they didn't fall across her cheek.

It took a little while before the memory came flooding back. It was just that kind of day. Finally, Wes shook his head. "You and that guy. The Midwestern guy. You had such a connection..."

Beatrice scrunched up her face. It was like she'd just had an epiphany. "That guy? What was his name again?" She pondered for a moment and then shrugged. "Gosh, he was arrogant. Wasn't he arrogant?"

Wes gaped at her, genuinely flabbergasted. From what he remembered, Beatrice and that Midwestern man had had the kind of chemistry you built your life upon.

"When you left the dinner, I got up and searched for you," Beatrice confessed after that. "I made someone scour the men's restroom just to see if you were around. Gosh, I was terrified. After a while, I got up the nerve to call your phone, but it was off."

Wes shook his head, imagining the scene. He'd thought she'd forgotten about him.

"I texted Lola the next day," Beatrice went on. "She was with you at lunch. She said something like, 'He's fine! How are you?' I didn't let on about what had happened. I didn't think your daughters had any right to know about our drama."

Wes wanted to thank her for that, but he stumbled over his words. "I don't know what to say..."

"Don't say anything," Beatrice told him.

Wes stared at the floor, listening to the tick-tick of the clock on the wall. Already, they'd lost so much time. He was nearly seventy, for goodness sake. Perhaps they had just a few years before his brain turned fully to mush.

And that, he knew, was lucky, in and of itself. His nephew, Steve, had lost his wife. They'd been terribly young. You weren't promised any amount of time. You had to be grateful for what you had.

Wes willed himself to get up the nerve to speak. *Wasn't he a man? Hadn't he raised three daughters? Hadn't he managed the Sunrise Cove Inn for many decades? Why had he lost his courage?*

"Beatrice," Wes managed to breathe.

Beatrice blinked those big, blue eyes at him. She seemed captivated by him. *Was it possible?*

"I'm falling for you," Wes told her, his words timid. "And it terrifies me. I do what I can when it comes to my dementia. I try to write everything down. I try to stay really organized. But I'm not so sure it's always possible. That's how I ended up here today. Something inside of me guided me here without letting me know."

Beatrice pressed her lips together. Wes was terrified she would tell him that it was all too much for her. He would understand.

But instead, Beatrice reached across her desk and

gathered both of Wes's hands in hers. She looked timid and alive, not unlike a young woman on the precipice of the rest of her life.

"I'm falling for you, too," Beatrice whispered. "And it doesn't mean I'm not scared. Gosh, I'm scared. But knowing that we have limited time? It makes every moment more precious to me."

Wes knelt his head and dropped a kiss on Beatrice's hand. His heart pounded so loudly that he couldn't hear himself think. Beatrice placed a hand on his head and lowered it to his neck, cradling him. For what seemed like a beautiful infinity, they held one another like that—facing whatever came next.

Wes couldn't help but wonder: *would they ever live together? Would they ever be intimate? Would they ever say, "I love you," like he and Anna once had?*

But these were questions for another time. Just then, all he could do was be grateful. All he could do was live in the now. That was all he had.

Chapter Nineteen

Charlotte sat cross-legged on the couch, her laptop across her lap. Classical music twinkled lightly from the speaker as she wrote an email to a new client, a bride who, against all odds, actually seemed to love her fiancé in a way that seemed real and powerful. When Charlotte had asked her, "What is your vision for your wedding?" the bride had blushed and said, "Gosh. I just want to spend the rest of my life with him. Can you make up the rest?"

Charlotte was more than willing to figure that out.

Just as Charlotte hit SEND, the front door burst open to reveal Rachel. Rachel looked her best that afternoon. She wore a jean miniskirt and a long-sleeved blouse with a pair of cowboy boots that she called "cowboy chic." Charlotte said, "I wish someone would have told me how to dress in high school. You seem to have your fashion down pat."

Rachel laughed and kicked off her cowboy boots. "What's that look you've gone with today? Sweatpants chic?"

Charlotte stuck out her tongue and tapped the couch cushion beside her. She pressed SEND and then closed her laptop, committed to another phase of the night. Rachel fell against her, burrowing herself against Charlotte's shoulder and arm. In the wake of Laura's death, there had been a huge number of Rachel-Charlotte snuggles. Never enough, of course. There never could be.

"How was your day, honey?" Charlotte whispered, tapping her lips against Rachel's head.

Rachel lifted her right shoulder into a shrug. Charlotte was again seized with worry. Just because the family had been through so much drama in the past couple of weeks didn't mean that Rachel's high school chaos hadn't depleted. *Had Charlotte missed something else? What could she possibly do?*

Charlotte rubbed Rachel's shoulder and cooed, "I'm starving. Do you want pizza and breadsticks?'

Rachel's lips curled into a smile. "I thought you'd never ask."

Twenty-five minutes later, a teenage boy with three juicy-looking pimples arrived with their pizza. Charlotte thanked him and tipped him big-time. As the door closed, Rachel admitted that the teenager was in her Geography class.

"He's quiet," Rachel said as she opened the pizza box. "Keeps to himself."

Charlotte crossed her legs again, watching her daughter. "And you? What are you?"

Rachel shrugged and took a slice, taking a bite. Her eyes closed as the cheese took hold of her. Charlotte had to laugh, tossing her head back. For a brief moment, she almost felt that both she and Rachel were young and on the cusp of the rest of their lives— both willing to eat pizza for every meal and dream up new ways to survive.

But it wasn't true. Charlotte had to guide her daughter, no matter what.

After Rachel nibbled half a slice, she grabbed the remote and headed for her favorite home improvement show. In this episode, a married couple talked about how they'd decided not to have children and instead focus all their time and effort on building "the perfect home."

"That's probably how you and Everett will be after I head to college," Rachel said as she took another bite.

Charlotte's stomach twisted. After a dramatic pause, she dropped forward to place one-half of her pizza on the cardboard. Rachel eyed her, confused.

"What is it?" Rachel demanded.

Charlotte had been avoiding this topic of conversation since she and Everett had discussed it at length two nights before. In truth, her insides were bungled up with grief.

"I don't know how to tell you this," Charlotte said, wiping her fingers on a napkin.

"Just say it." Rachel's tone was sharp and angry.

Charlotte understood: Rachel was tired of surprises. Most surprises in her world were negative. She was always prepared for a new attack.

"Everett's been offered a new job on Orcas Island," Charlotte said. She was surprised at how easily she said it, hardly with a crack in her voice. It was almost as though she spoke of the weather.

Rachel's jaw dropped. She whacked her thigh angrily. "You're kidding."

Charlotte shook her head, her eyes to the couch cushion. "Everett has worked so, so hard to build his career.

When I first met him, he was taking photographs of events. That wasn't his calling! It never was."

Rachel stuttered. "He used you. He used that event to gain notoriety."

Charlotte wanted to compliment her daughter on using the word "notoriety" but held herself back. It wasn't the time.

"He did not use me," Charlotte shot back.

"So what? Is the engagement just off, now?" Rachel demanded. She leaped from the couch and staggered back, pizza forgotten.

"No!" Charlotte cried, surprised at how passionate she suddenly felt. "Everett and I are going to find a way to get through this."

"How?" Rachel demanded. She blinked back tears. "I mean, next year when I head off to college? What are you going to do? Are you going to just be in this stupid house alone? This isn't even the house that you and Dad raised me in! It was supposed to be where you and Everett grew old together!"

With that, Rachel burst into tears. She placed her face, a red-hot tomato, in her palms and shook with sorrow. Charlotte jumped from the couch and wrapped her body around her, protecting her. Had an avalanche fallen over them from above, Rachel would have been protected.

"Shh," Charlotte cooed. "It's okay. I'm not going to be alone."

In truth, Charlotte had no idea if that was correct. But she had to believe in it just then, if only for Rachel's sake.

After a long, loud, and sorrowful five minutes, Charlotte leaned back and gazed into Rachel's eyes. She was her perfect daughter, her everything.

"I love you, Rachel. You know that I love you more than any creature on earth."

Rachel nodded, biting her lower lip.

"No matter what happens between Everett and I, I want you to know that our relationship will always be my very first priority," Charlotte continued, swiping a tear from her cheek. "I promise you that."

Rachel blinked back tears. Slowly, she shifted up onto the couch again and steadied herself. The pizza remained before them, still with five slices, ready to be eaten.

"I'm sorry for acting like that," Rachel said suddenly. She sounded more like an adult than a teenager. "I don't know why I freaked out. That's your business, your life. I shouldn't be so possessive about something that isn't mine."

Charlotte was at a loss for words. She cocked her head, trying to drum up some response. But instead, she took a slice of pizza, took a bite, and watched the home improvement show on television for a solid five minutes. Throughout, they took sledgehammers to the dilapidated pool in the backyard, casting gunk across the yard.

For the first time, Charlotte understood what Rachel had meant. The violence looked necessary. She would have liked to destroy something.

When enough time had passed, Charlotte dared herself to ask the question that had been heavy on her mind for what seemed like years by then.

"Now that I've told you my secret, will you please tell me what's been going on at school? I've been so worried about you."

To Charlotte's surprise, Rachel didn't overreact to the question. She heaved a sigh and set down her half-eaten slice of pizza, wiping her fingers across another napkin.

"It sounds so stupid, now," Rachel said.

"If it's stupid, we can laugh about it," Charlotte told her.

Rachel coughed into her hand as her eyes glazed over. "Okay. Just. Please, don't judge me too hard for it?"

"I never would."

"Okay. Well, at the end of summer, I went to a beach party," Rachel began, her nostrils flared. "And Chad was there. He's this guy at school. I mean, not just any guy. He's popular."

Charlotte wanted to tell Rachel how little popularity mattered in high school, but she held it back.

"But the thing is, he's been dating Gretchen Magnum for like four years," Rachel continued. "They broke up this summer— it was a huge drama. And on that night of the party, Chad came over to me and wanted to talk."

Charlotte could feel the excitement behind Rachel's voice. It was clear that this night had changed Rachel's life.

"We talked for like a half-hour. Maybe forty-five minutes. Maybe," Rachel continued, her cheeks reddening. "But a week or so later, Chad and Gretchen got back together, and Gretchen decided to make my life a living hell. All because I talked to her boyfriend at a stupid party!"

Rachel hung her head. Shame marked its way across her face. Charlotte's heart ballooned. In some ways, this story was far less dramatic than she'd thought it would be. This was a strange relief (even though she knew just how "big" this felt in Rachel's world).

"Oh, honey," Charlotte whispered as she crossed the boundary between them and held Rachel in her arms again. "I hate that this girl did this to you."

"I did it," Rachel hiccupped. "I flirted with him."

Charlotte stepped back, shaking her head. "All you did was talk to a boy who you thought was cute. That is not a crime. Do you understand me? You did nothing wrong."

Rachel's chin wiggled with sorrow. It was clear that she carried this guilt around with her; she regretted the party with everything she had.

But to Charlotte, life was too short for such regrets.

"Honey, you have to look this Gretchen girl straight in the face and tell her to leave you alone," Charlotte said suddenly. "Tell her what you told me— that you didn't do anything wrong. Her stupid boyfriend was talking to you first, not the other way around."

Charlotte felt resolute. Slowly, Rachel lifted her eyes to her mother's and gave her a firm nod. It felt like they'd just made a pact— one that solidified the strength they would use for the rest of their lives.

"I'll do it," Rachel breathed. "I promise."

Charlotte swallowed the lump in her throat. "You deserve to be treated like the queen that you are. Never forget that."

Chapter Twenty

The soft purr of the motor was the only sound. Together, Charlotte and Steve sat staring straight ahead, hovering in the parking lot in front of the grief counselor's office. Once upon a time, after a very different death, this very grief counselor had helped walk Charlotte from the darkness of her own mind. Charlotte stopped the engine and bowed her head, sensing Steve's hesitation.

"I understand why you don't want to go," she whispered.

Steve groaned, kneading his thighs with both hands. "I just feel so foolish."

"You shouldn't." Charlotte swallowed the lump in her throat and glanced at her older brother, who'd lost so much weight that he no longer looked quite like himself. "She just gives you the tools to keep going. It's up to you to use those tools."

Steve coughed twice. He'd already confessed several times over the previous few weeks that he struggled knowing how to go on. If it wasn't for Isabella, who had remained at home, Steve probably wouldn't have kept himself together half as well. Given his current state, that was difficult to imagine.

"Laura wouldn't want this," Charlotte said under her breath, watching as the key jangled back and forth in the ignition. "She would want you to keep fighting. To keep living."

It was a low blow, and Charlotte knew that. Still, she just wanted Steve to fight for something.

Steve grumbled and rubbed his right eye with a fist. After a dramatic pause, he shoved himself through the door and stepped up on the curb. Charlotte's heart dropped. How she wanted to take his pain away; how she wanted to turn back time and deliver him to another era, one in which Laura lived on forever.

It wasn't meant to be.

* * *

It was hard to believe it was already October. Laura had been gone for over a month, leaving them all reeling and searching for meaning in the midst of a chaotic and meaningless time. Weeks had paraded them forward into the oranges, browns, and yellows of autumn.

Charlotte parked at the coffee shop a few blocks down from the grief counselor's office. There, she purchased a latte with oat milk and sat, staring out at the impenetrable fog as it built itself up over the Vineyard Sound. As she sipped the creamy coffee, she racked her brain for some memory of what she'd told the grief counselor about her own grief process. "I keep thinking he's going to walk back through the front door, and everything will go back to how it always was," she'd once said. Gosh, she'd felt so foolish after that. But the grief counselor had told her, point blank, that it was better to get those words out.

As Charlotte sat, two figures appeared in the fog, growing closer and closer. Their hands were clasped together as they waded their way toward the coffee shop. Suddenly, Charlotte jolted up with recognition.

"Uncle Wes! Hello!" Charlotte waved a hand as he entered, holding the door open for Beatrice.

Beatrice tidied her hair with a wave of her hand and smiled warmly, her blue eyes glittering. Across her chest, binoculars bounced gently.

"Hi, Charlotte. What a surprise." Wes beamed as they approached. His color had returned to him in recent weeks, and even his stomach had filled out a bit— probably from a healthy appetite. That was the thing about new relationships, no matter your age. You wanted to do everything together: eat, sleep, dream, and, in this case, birdwatch.

"How is it out there? Doesn't look like the visibility is that great," Charlotte said.

Beatrice nodded, her eyes tracing back toward Wes. "The fog came just as soon as we stepped out the door."

"I pestered her for a cup of coffee and a scone," Wes said, his smile widening.

"Yes. You know me, Wes. You always have to twist my arm to get me to go along with sweets in the middle of the afternoon," Beatrice teased.

Wes blushed and palmed his neck. Charlotte could half-imagine them as teenagers, both anxious about saying the right thing.

As Beatrice headed up to order their coffees and

baked goods, Wes bent his head to say, "Kerry told me that Steve has his first grief counseling appointment today."

Charlotte nodded. "It took some serious prodding to get him to go."

"I can imagine. A man like Steve is often too proud for something like that," Wes said. "I hope he knows he's doing the right thing."

"More than that, I just hope it helps," Charlotte whispered.

Beatrice returned, folding a receipt and slipping it into her jeans pocket. She lifted her eyes to Wes again, holding him in her gaze as though he was the most important person in her universe. Thus far, gossip surrounding the new couple had gone like this: they'd told no one when they'd begun their relationship, but it was clear that they were now (finally) together.

Apparently, Wes had told Lola privately, "I don't know how long we'll have together, but I plan to use every second that God has gifted me with this beautiful, intelligent woman."

It was his own version of a second chance. Charlotte supposed everyone was allowed that, no matter their age.

"And how is Everett doing out west?" Wes asked, his voice brightening. "Audrey showed me some of the photographs he's published for that magazine. Wow! The nature out there is spectacular."

"We were researching the birds found on Orcas Island," Beatrice said conspiratorially. "Perhaps Everett could show us around if we planned a visit."

Charlotte's cheeks burned, just as they always did when one of her family members brought up the issue of Everett's departure.

"He's doing so well," Charlotte affirmed with the flip of her hair. "His editor has fallen in love with his work and demands more and more of him. His career is like a shooting star."

Beatrice nodded. "And yours, as well. I read yet another article about you in a wedding magazine."

Charlotte laughed. "I saw that. I couldn't believe that particular bride gave me such a rave review. We definitely had our differences throughout the course of the wedding planning."

Wes arched an eyebrow. "Was that the woman who threw a hissy fit in the middle of the wedding, only for her husband to shove cake in her face?"

"The very one," Charlotte said, impressed.

Beatrice howled and smacked her thigh. "You're kidding!"

Wes lifted a worn-looking brown book and waved it. "I wrote that story in my diary the minute I heard it. I was skimming through my notes from the summer just last night when I came across it. I had a good laugh."

The coffee barista called Beatrice back to grab her order. This left just Wes and Charlotte, who gave one another tender smiles and prepared to say goodbye. Just before Charlotte headed back into the fog, however, Wes hesitated.

"I know you must be broken up about Everett taking that job," he began.

Charlotte began to protest but soon dropped her head, resigned. "I haven't been handling it well."

Wes clucked his tongue. "When Everett looks at you, he sees the sun and the moon and the stars. It's something a man like me understands. He wouldn't have gone out there if he thought he would lose you in the process."

Charlotte furrowed her brow. What did that mean?

"You'll find a way to build a life together," Wes continued. "Because when two people find one another the way you and Everett did, you know better than to throw it away."

Beatrice returned, a platter of scones balanced perfectly across the flat of her hand and two handles of mugs wrapped tightly in her other. Charlotte sensed this sentiment was related to Wes's own life; he knew better than to throw away his relationship with Beatrice, despite his dementia diagnosis and the lateness of their years.

Charlotte bid them both goodbye and headed back into the foggy afternoon. Her breath was quick, adding its own fog to the muck of the air. Once at her vehicle, a text rang through her cell. It was from Rachel.

> RACHEL: Mom! We've got an SOS situation at the boutique.

> RACHEL: Seriously! Get over here as soon as you can.

Charlotte's eyes bugged out. Frightened, she dialed her daughter, who answered on the second ring.

"Rachel? Are you okay?"

Rachel's laughter rocketed through the phone. Immediately, Charlotte was able to breathe again.

"I'm fine! I mean, sort of. Gail, Abby, and I are at Kelli and Lexi's boutique, trying and failing to pick out our Homecoming dresses."

Charlotte's lips curved into a smile. This was the sort of thing she'd dreamed of when she'd thought of Rachel's senior year. This was Charlotte's time to shine.

"I just have to pick up and drop off your Uncle Steve

before I meet you," Charlotte explained. "I'll be there in ten, maybe fifteen. Can you hold out till then?"

"We'll try," Rachel quipped.

Charlotte hovered outside the grief counselor's office, her hands on ten and two. Slowly, Steve limped from the building, his hands shoved in his pockets. When he finally reached the passenger seat of Charlotte's car, he fell back as though he'd lost all control of his arms and legs.

For a long time, Charlotte wasn't sure what to say. *Could she ask him what had happened? Could she ask if anything had helped?*

But finally, just as Charlotte's panic mounted to a terrific height, Steve exhaled all the air from his lungs and said in a very quiet voice, "I think I like her. I think I like her a lot."

Charlotte was so relieved. She changed gears in the car and began to creep toward the main road, her heart pounding.

"Today was really just introductory," Steve continued, scratching his beard. "I told her it's a huge experiment for me, telling someone so much about myself. So, we started small. I hardly spoke about Laura at all. I guess because it still seems too personal."

"That makes sense," Charlotte affirmed. "You're strangers. But in a few weeks..."

"I know. I can already tell how open she is," Steve explained. "And— well. Maybe this is stupid to say. But I do feel guilty, laying the burden of my emotions on you and Isabella and Jonathon all the time. The grief counselor is literally there to receive those emotions and teach me how to handle them. The guilty feeling isn't there when I'm with her. It's remarkable."

Charlotte stopped at a stop sign and glanced over at

her dear elder brother, whose skin seemed to shine with renewed health. This, she knew, was the power of conversation. It couldn't be discredited.

Steve continued to chat about his opinions on counseling and his previous-held notions surrounding therapy in general. "I couldn't have been more incorrect," he said.

A couple of minutes later, Steve asked Charlotte what she was up to the rest of the day. "I feel like I want to be out and about," he explained. "I don't know if I can sit in front of the television for another night."

Charlotte gave him a curious look. "I don't suppose you'd like to help me with a very important task?"

"Anything," Steve told her firmly. "I'll help you with anything you need."

Charlotte's grin widened. "I hope you don't regret that."

"Uh oh. Should I be worried?"

Five minutes later, Charlotte parked the car outside of Kelli's boutique. Steve scratched his head and followed her up the porch steps and into the vintage boutique, where Kelli's daughter, Lexi, currently worked the counter. In the corner, Gail, Abby, and Rachel stood in three outrageous-looking dresses. Rachel's had a train about six feet long, while Gail looked like she was an extra in an eighties music video. Abby, on the other hand, looked Amish.

"Uncle Steve!" the girls cried in unison, clasping their hands.

Steve barked with surprised laughter. "What on earth are you girls wearing?"

Rachel sighed, exasperated. Her eyes bugged out as she said, "See, Mom? We've needed your help the whole time. We're at a loss."

"It's worse than I thought," Charlotte teased, dropping down to lift the train of Rachel's dress far into the air before dropping it back down. "Are you going for Princess Diana?"

Rachel's cheeks were tomato red. "I don't know what I'm going for. But I'm freaking out."

"Honey, don't worry yourself so much," Charlotte told her. Her hand on her hips, she added, "You told me that you weren't even going to go to the Homecoming Dance this year. What changed?"

Gail and Abby exchanged glances and then burst into giggles. Behind Charlotte, Steve joined the laughter, whipping his hand through his graying curls. The laughter was such a surprise compared to the darkness of the previous month. Charlotte had to smile.

"Girls? Are you ever going to tell us what's up?" Charlotte demanded.

Gail snorted with laughter as Abby found a way to compose herself. Rachel gave her a nervous smile and a shrug. Obviously, she wanted someone else to explain.

"Rachel stood up to Gretchen," Abby said under her breath. It was almost like Rachel had stood up to an evil villain or a mass murderer. That was how impressive it seemed.

Charlotte cocked her head, eyeing her daughter. "What happened?"

"She was ripping into her again," Gail continued. "About what happened over the summer. She kept asking her who she thought she was and why she thought she deserved attention from someone like Chad."

"And suddenly, Rachel stepped forward, pointed her finger in Gretchen's face, and said..." Abby gestured toward Rachel to say what she'd said.

Rachel puffed out her cheeks. "Guys. It's embarrassing."

"It's not!" Gail cried. Her eyes on Charlotte, she spoke for her. "She told Gretchen to get the heck out of her face—"

"Except she didn't say heck," Abby reminded her.

"And that Chad was a kind, considerate, and intelligent guy. That he deserved someone much better than Gretchen. Someone who actually knew where Tunisia was on the map," Gail said.

"Which was a low blow, given the fact that Gretchen is pretty awful at Geography and had recently messed up that question on the exam," Abby continued.

Rachel snickered, swaying her arms forward and back.

"But that's not all," Gail said in singsong.

"Chad heard all of it!" Rachel cried, unable to contain her excitement a moment longer. "And by the end of the day, he'd broken up with Gretchen. It was a huge scandal. Gretchen hates me even more than before, but she doesn't have power over me. It's the most amazing feeling..."

"Rachel!" Uncle Steve cried, stepping forward to shake her hand. "I don't think I've heard of such a big act of bravery in many years. It's like something out of a movie. Congratulations."

"And now, the whole school is gossiping about how Chad said he might want to dance with Rachel at Homecoming," Abby cried.

"And Gretchen's head is going to explode," Gail affirmed.

Rachel waved a hand. "If Chad asks me to dance, he asks me to dance. I don't care either way."

But you could see it in the glow of her eyes. Obviously, she wanted to be asked. Every girl wanted to be asked. It was just the law of high school, one that never really changed.

Over the next two hours, Steve and Charlotte sat on a bench in the boutique and "judged" the multiple homecoming dresses that Rachel, Gail, and Abby donned throughout the evening. Despite Steve's mechanic training, he had a pretty stellar eye and normally went for more classically cut pieces, while Charlotte normally judged with trends in mind.

By closing time, all three senior girls had selected their dresses. Rachel had opted for an asymmetrically cut turquoise dress with tiny buttons up the back. Charlotte had voted for this one, especially because it was the sort of dress you couldn't get away with wearing any other time of your life. It was a seventeen-year-old's dress, and that's what made it so special.

Gail and Abby had each gone with Steve's recommendation, with Abby wearing a classic black with a high neckline and Gail in a tutu dress with thin straps.

"If I tell Claire that you helped pick these out, she'll probably faint," Charlotte teased Steve as they walked out, the dresses slung across their arms.

"I'd love to see her face," Steve admitted with a laugh.

Behind them, the teenagers gabbed about the upcoming Homecoming Dance, skipping lightly beneath an October moon. The fog had cleared, casting the island in fresh darkness. Spontaneously, Charlotte leaped for her brother and hugged him tightly, so grateful that they'd been able to spend this night together.

With Everett half a world away and Laura gone a

month, the siblings needed one another more than ever. They were picking up the pieces of their lives, attempting to put things right again. Probably what would come of it wouldn't resemble anything they'd had before. That, Charlotte knew, would have to be okay.

Chapter Twenty-One

EVERETT: Send me pictures!

EVERETT: And tell that Chad guy I've got
my eye on him. One wrong move, and
he's done for.

Charlotte chuckled to herself, texting Everett with a big grin plastered across her face. Upstairs, Rachel, Gail, and Abby finished up their Homecoming Dance look, hopefully leaning more toward "subtle" rather than "Kardashian" when it came to makeup. Charlotte didn't have any say in the matter. The girls were seventeen, ready for the rest of their lives. They would have to make their own makeup mistakes along the way. Charlotte certainly had.

Claire and Steve hustled into Charlotte's living room, carrying margaritas.

"Isn't this so exciting?" Claire cried, clearly on the verge of actual tears.

"It's not even prom yet," Charlotte teased her. "You'll be a mess by then."

Steve passed a margarita to Charlotte and lifted his high for the other sisters to cheer. Although Charlotte couldn't be sure, she thought Steve looked a little bit fuller in the cheeks than he had a week or two ago. It had now been six weeks since Laura's death. Perhaps he'd found a way to sustain himself again, bit-by-bit.

"Mmm. Delicious," Charlotte said as she took in the tang of the margarita.

"You can thank the margarita mix I bought at the store for that," Claire joked.

"Claire! They're so easy to make homemade," Charlotte said.

"Lay off," Steve teased. "You said already that they're delicious. What else do you want? So pretentious." He shook his head, his smile mischievous.

Charlotte laughed, tossing her head back. There was something about a joke from her older brother just then. He had to push himself harder than ever to make one, which made her appreciate it all the more.

Rachel, Gail, and Abby appeared downstairs in their Homecoming Dresses a few minutes later. Their makeup was on the very edge of "too much," but Charlotte, Claire, and Steve could give them nothing but compliments.

"The most beautiful girls in school!" Uncle Steve called.

"All three of you get my vote for Homecoming Queen!" Claire quipped.

"Your dates are lucky..." Charlotte said, eyeing the door.

The doorbell rang. Charlotte stepped toward it, only to have Rachel whisk her way forward, her turquoise dress flailing out behind her like the sail of a sailboat. She opened it with the pep of a teenage girl and then seemed immediately embarrassed and shy. The contrast was alarming.

On the other side of the door stood a handsome teenage boy in a tuxedo, his hands folded over his waist. Based on photographs Charlotte had seen on Rachel's social media, this was Chad himself— a boy who had recently confessed that actually, he'd always had a crush on Rachel. Charlotte had pleaded with Rachel not to rush into anything, especially given the fact that Chad's ex had made her life a living hell the past couple of months. To this, Rachel had said, "That's ancient history, Mom."

Times changed quickly in high school. Charlotte should have remembered that.

Chad greeted Charlotte with a firm handshake. For a strange moment, Charlotte half-imagined Jason stepping out of the kitchen to meet the boy for the first time. *How would Jason have handled any of this? Would he have been happy with how Charlotte had done?*

"Hi. I'm Uncle Steve," Steve said to Chad, shaking his hand.

"And I'm Aunt Claire," Claire said, her voice a little high-pitched.

It was a funny thing that adults could get nervous in front of teenagers. Charlotte could attest that it was true. She felt it even now as her stomach flipped over.

"Let's get some shots of the two of you," she instructed Rachel and Chad. They stood near the fireplace, with Chad's hand on Rachel's lower back. *Was it too low? How was any mother supposed to know what was right?*

Charlotte took several pictures while her eyes were glossy with tears. Mid-way through the final round, the teens looked fidgety and anxious. Gail and Abby's dates arrived, one in an orange tux and the other in a blue one. Gail and Abby howled with laughter and explained they were all going as "just friends." The four of them took outrageous photographs that had Steve, Charlotte, and Claire practically on their knees with laughter.

By the time six o'clock hit, Charlotte found herself in her socks on the front porch, waving manically as her baby girl drove off with a teenage boy. Once upon a time, Charlotte had done the same with Jason Hamner.

What a beautiful thing to have the honor of watching your baby girl grow up.

It was one of the greatest gifts of life. Charlotte knew that.

Back inside, Steve fetched them more margaritas, and Claire turned on the speaker system to Fleetwood Mac's *Rumours*. As "Dreams" kicked off, Charlotte lifted her arms to the sky and wailed, "Now here you go again, you say you want your freedom. Well, who am I to keep you down?"

"Dang. That's fitting," Claire said, lifting her margarita. "Not only for the girls but for Everett, too."

Charlotte scrunched her nose and blinked back tears. "I'm so glad you guys are here. The house would feel so empty without you."

Everett and Claire exchanged glances. In the background, Stevie Nicks continued to wail in that broken-hearted way of hers.

Suddenly, Claire reached for her purse and dragged out an envelope. Her eyes were cloudy, her face pinched. It was exactly the face she often made when she wanted so desperately to keep a secret but couldn't.

"Charlotte," Claire began.

"Claire?" she shot back.

"Well. Um." Claire shook her head. "Steve and I got together and talked about your current situation. And how you've been putting yourself out there for the family so much the past few months."

Charlotte shook her head. "We've all been there for each other, in every way."

"Yes. Yes. You're right." Claire sniffed as she passed over the envelope. "But Steve and I wanted to gift you this. You aren't allowed to refuse it, okay?"

Charlotte arched her brow as she slowly opened the envelope. She flipped it to tap out a single boarding pass—one that read: BOSTON to SEATTLE. It was dated for the following day.

Charlotte lifted her head up with surprise. "What is this?"

Steve stuttered slightly with his answer. "I told Claire I didn't think you'd push yourself to go visit him soon enough because you felt you were needed here."

"It's not that I feel that I'm needed here..." Charlotte began.

"I know. I know." Steve forced himself to look her in the eye. "You've been there for me in every conceivable way since Laura died. I can honestly say that I wouldn't have gotten this far without you, and I know that I won't make it to next year without your strength, your advice, and your guidance. But Charlotte, you have to take care of yourself, too. We all see that."

Claire nodded vigorously beside him, clasping her hands.

Charlotte bit her lower lip, overwhelmed with feeling. "I can't accept this."

"You can and you will," Claire instructed. "You know that I adore having Rachel around the house. Besides, she'll hardly notice you're gone. She'll be busy gossiping about the dance."

Charlotte flung herself across the room and wrapped her arms around her brother and her sister. The boarding pass remained locked in her right hand. So soon, she would see her love again. So soon, they would hold each other close and whisper their every thought as their laughter cascaded across the waters of the West Sound and across the mighty Pacific.

* * *

The flight path from Boston to Seattle was not an easy one. Charlotte, who wasn't exactly a frequent flyer, struggled with security and was ultimately forced to throw away a huge bottle of conditioner. *Why had she packed that?* Obviously, she'd lost her head. She tried to explain how nervous she was to the airline security worker, but the woman just waved her aside, rolling her eyes. In the bathroom, Charlotte laughed to herself and touched up her makeup.

"Nobody else cares that you're in love, Char," she muttered to herself, swiping mascara across her eyelashes. "Keep your mouth shut."

Oh, but she couldn't stop smiling. During the entire six-hour flight from Boston to Seattle, she alternated between reading and daydreaming, her gaze locked on the puffy clouds outside. It seemed insane that people had ever learned how to fly. Now, it was an everyday thing, like driving a car or walking to the store.

In reality, it was a miracle. More people should have been talking about that.

Once Charlotte landed in Seattle, she waited for her

black suitcase and checked up on photos from the Home-coming Dance, all of which Rachel had sent her that morning from Claire's place. Most of them were silly; some were sweet. In one, Chad kissed Rachel's cheek delicately as she made a funny face. Charlotte's heart seized.

Yet again, she faced reality: just next year, Rachel would have a life of her own. Probably, that life would be off the island.

Charlotte rented a car from the airport and headed north to the ferry. The drive took a full three hours, but she powered through with a series of playlists of nineties songs and a radio station that played hits from the Pacific Northwest. Back in the day, Kurt Cobain had been every nineties high schooler's idol. Back then, Charlotte had pictured him in the haze of the Pacific Northwest, stewing in poetry and killer guitar licks.

Gosh, that had been so long ago.

What a tragedy that he'd died so young. What a tragedy that so many people across the world still missed him— not his fans, but his mother, his child. Charlotte had never listened to Nirvana in that headspace before. It wasn't comfortable. It reminded her of how old she was and just how grateful she was to be so old.

On the ferry, Charlotte leaped from the rental vehicle and rushed to the top deck. There, another rain was frantic, echoing across the hood of her jacket. The rain slicked down and fell to her feet.

Most others on the ferry huddled inside, but she wanted to stand at the edge and watch the rushing water as she grew closer and closer to her love.

Just as he'd said he would, Everett awaited her at the docks. He, too, wore a thick raincoat, and his hair and beard were a bit longer than normal, proof that the Pacific Northwest had gotten into his veins. Forgetting her car altogether, Charlotte rushed down the ramp on foot and flung herself into his arms. He whirled her around and around as her shrieks rang out across the quiet island.

He was her home.

She knew that now.

After they retrieved her car, he drove them back to the cabin he'd rented during his stay on the island. He talked about how marvelous it had been to dig into the dynamic mysteries of Orcas Island.

"You would have loved this older woman, Char. She's made hundreds of quilts, all by hand. I hardly knew what to ask her and thought to myself, 'Gosh, Charlotte should be here.'"

Charlotte's heart swelled with love.

The cabin was little more than a living room attached to a kitchen, plus an upstairs where Everett's king-sized bed was now covered in one of that older woman's hand-stitched quilts. From the front window, you could peer northwest, toward what Everett said was the "invisible waterline between Canada and the United States." Charlotte felt as though she and Everett sat on the edge of the world together.

True to his newfound "Pacific Northwest Mountain Man" status, Everett built a fire in the fireplace. In minutes, it crackled and spat, its orange flames licking the bricks. Charlotte sat in front of the fire cross-legged, watching him work and listening to the tap-tap of the rain outside. For the first time in ages, her soul felt quiet.

"I've missed you," she confessed, her voice breaking.

Everett turned and knelt beside her. He held her

hand gently as he said, "I haven't been the same without you."

For a long time, they were silent. Charlotte wanted to tell him everything— that she'd been afraid that they wouldn't be able to make the distance work; that she'd thought he would have already met someone else by then; that she'd assumed she could slip back into her Martha's Vineyard life without him.

But the only inevitable thing, she knew, was change.

Before Charlotte had the chance to speak, Everett said, "I think it's working, though. The distance. But I couldn't and wouldn't do it forever."

"Rachel's applying for colleges," Charlotte whispered. "My family is patching itself up. And they assure me that they don't need me that much anymore, no matter how much it hurts me to hear that. The world always finds a way of moving on without you."

"Not me," Everett told her firmly. "I'm moving on with you. Not without."

Charlotte's throat tightened. Outside, a shiver of lightning flashed across the sky.

Slowly, Charlotte reached for her backpack, unzipped it, and removed a stack of magazines. Everett watched her, mystified. But slowly, a realization came over him.

"We'll marry on Martha's Vineyard," he said softly.

Charlotte blinked back tears. "We'll marry on Martha's Vineyard. Next summer or the one after that."

"And then, we'll build our lives here."

"I looked into the wedding industry out here," Charlotte continued, giving him a crooked smile. "Turns out, loads of couples need wedding planners out here in the San Juan islands, as well."

"I guess someone had better help them," Everett said.

After that, Everett curled himself around her, his muscular legs on either side of her slight ones and his strong arms around her stomach. He pressed his scratchy beard against her cheek, and she shrieked playfully, calling him "Paul Bunyan." He burrowed against her, saying, "You like it."

Charlotte laughed good-naturedly, feeling light as air. The flames popped and spat as the logs continued to crisp. It was terribly hard to quantify the events of her life — from meeting Jason to giving birth to watching everything fall apart. Bit-by-bit, she'd stumbled her way toward this marvelous future. A part of her wanted to contain the here-and-now, hold it in her hands, and keep it. But another part reminded her of the beauty of constant change. There was no telling what came next. That was the best part.

Coming Next

Start Reading a Vineyard Spring

Other Books by Katie Winters

The Vineyard Sunset Series

Secrets of Mackinac Island Series

Sisters of Edgartown Series

A Katama Bay Series

A Mount Desert Island Series

A Nantucket Sunset Series

Made in the USA
Columbia, SC
12 July 2023

20301873R00117